ZOMBIE HALLOWEEN

GOOSEBUMPS HorrorLand™

Also Available from Scholastic Audio Books

Goosebumps®

MOST WANTED

SPECIAL EDITION

ZOMBIE HALLOWEEN

R.L. STINE

SCHOLASTIC INC.

ISBN 978-0-545-62776-4

Goosebumps book series created by Parachute Press, Inc.
Copyright © 2014 by Scholastic Inc.

12 11 10 9 8 7 6 5 4 3 2   14 15 16 17 18 19/0

Printed in the U.S.A.
First printing, July 2014

WELCOME. YOU ARE MOST WANTED.

Come in. I'm R.L. Stine. Welcome to the Goosebumps office.

Glad you made it through the barbed wire fence. Don't worry. Those cuts will stop bleeding in an hour or two.

Why do we have a barbed wire fence? To keep the Abominable Snowman from escaping. I'm surprised you didn't see him. He's creeping up right behind you. Hurry. Step inside and shut the door. You don't want to find out why everyone calls him "Abominable."

Hey, don't be scared of Eddie over there. Eddie woke up dead tired one morning. Guess what? He actually was *dead*. Yes, Eddie is a zombie. But he doesn't like that word. He likes to be called "life-challenged."

He's not much trouble. He only needs to eat human flesh once a day. Don't be nervous. He just finished his breakfast.

Whom did he have for breakfast? I'm not sure. But I haven't seen my brother all morning. . . .

Eddie — what did I tell you about eating the family?

Oh, well. Let me ask you a question before Eddie has to have his next meal. What do you think is the Most Wanted holiday?

You're right. It's Halloween. It's the most fun night of the year. And . . . it can be the scariest.

A boy named Kenny Manzetti is going to tell you about his Halloween.

Kenny and his sister, Tricia, moved into a creepy old house that looked like it should be in a horror movie. They didn't believe all the scary stories they heard about the house. They decided to have a Halloween party to meet the kids in their new neighborhood. But they had some unexpected guests. . . .

You see, the house stood across the street from a graveyard. And some people buried there — hideous, rotting zombies — decided to make this a Zombie Halloween. . . .

PART ONE

1944

1

A chill rolled down my back as my friend Ivy and I gazed up at my new house. The house was dark gray with peeling paint. Black shutters tilted at the dust-smeared windows.

Under the sloping roof, one attic window was broken and covered with cardboard. The wind whistled into the window, high above our heads. It sounded like someone screaming.

I wanted to scream.

"It's a haunted house," I said. "It belongs in a horror movie."

"Your mom will get it cleaned up, Mario," Ivy said.

I knew Ivy for only a couple of weeks. She was the first friend I made since we moved to Franklin Village. She was cheerful Miss Sunshine all the time.

I told her that. She said, "I'd rather be Miss Sunshine than someone howling at the full moon."

Does that make any sense?

Ivy was always saying things like that. But I liked her anyway. She was cute. She was twelve, like me. Tiny, with a pointed chin and pointed little nose. Like an elf in the picture books my mom used to read me when I was little.

She had short blond hair and green eyes. And she usually wore the same green sweater with a lacy white collar. I guess because it matched her eyes.

"I couldn't get to sleep last night," I said. "I kept hearing a tap-tap-tap above me. I knew what it was. It was mice running across my ceiling."

"Tap-tap-tap is better than thump-thump-thump," Ivy said.

That made me laugh.

I turned away from the house. It made me sad that Mom and I had to live in such a creepy old wreck of a place. But we really had no choice.

My dad was in Germany fighting the war. And Mom was working two factory jobs to earn enough money for us to get by. I almost never saw her.

"You're the man of the house now, Mario," Mom told me the day we moved into this horrible place. "It's a tough time for everyone. And being gloomy isn't going to help."

"But Gloomy is my middle name," I said. "Mario Gloomy Manzetti."

I was trying to make her laugh. She hardly ever smiled these days, and she had these lines under her eyes she never had before.

6

She swept her black hair behind her shoulder. "Promise me you'll do your best," she said.

I raised my right hand and swore I'd do my best.

"We are lucky to have a house," Mom said.

"Lucky," I repeated.

She tugged at the brown leather bomber jacket I liked to wear because it made me look tough. "Mario, that jacket is getting small on you," she said.

"I'll try not to grow anymore," I told her. I tightened my stomach and hunched down to my knees.

That made her laugh.

Now, Ivy and I stood in front of the house with the October wind gusting around us. Fat brown leaves danced around our legs.

"I guess the worst part is living across the street from a graveyard," I said.

Ivy poked me in the ribs. "Are you scared?" she asked in a singsong voice. "Is little Mario scared of a graveyard?"

"I'm not scared," I said, poking her back. "It's just . . . depressing."

"Ooh. Big word," she said. "So? You live in a haunted house across the street from a grave-yard. What is the big deal?"

The truth is, maybe I *was* a little scared. I'm not a tough guy. Sometimes I have nightmares that make me wake up all sweaty and shaky.

And I've never been in a fight with another kid. I always find a way to talk my way out of fights.

When I was little, I pretended to be Superman or Captain Marvel, the new comic book heroes. I wore a towel for a cape and had my underpants over my pajama pants. And I ran around, pretending to "leap tall buildings in a single bound."

I think I really believed there were these powerful guys in capes and tights who were around to fight bad guys and protect everyone else. But then my dad went off to war, and I had to grow up a little and forget that comic book stuff.

Ivy leaned into the wind and trotted across the street, her blond hair bouncing behind her.

"Hey, wait up!" I shouted. "Where are you going?"

I could see where she was headed. Into the graveyard.

Our shoes crackled over the brown leaves as we followed a path through the tilted stone graves. Wind gusts made the old gravestones creak and groan.

"Why don't we go to the candy store instead?" I asked. I pointed to the little store on the corner past the graveyard. "I have a nickel. We could load up on root beer barrels and licorice sticks."

"Mom said not to ruin my appetite for dinner," Ivy said. "Don't you like walking in this place? Some of the graves are so old —"

"It's . . . my first time," I said.

The sky darkened. I looked up and saw storm clouds rolling overhead. The wind rattled the limbs of the old tree beside us.

I shivered. I raised the collar of my bomber jacket. My eyes gazed all around. The blowing, crackling leaves made the whole place seem *alive*.

Ivy pointed. "That grave is so tiny. Do you think a child is buried there?"

Before I could answer, I saw something that made me gasp.

I grabbed Ivy's arm. "Look. Ivy. Something just moved — by that tombstone."

We both stared into the gray light.

"Oh, noooo," I moaned.

I watched, trembling in horror as someone climbed out of a grave.

I squeezed Ivy's arm. We both froze and watched. Dressed all in black, the terrifying figure kept his face down. He stepped from behind the tall gravestone — raised his arms in front of him — and began staggering stiffly toward Ivy and me.

"Noooo. Oh, noooo." Another moan escaped my throat.

And then the staggering creature raised his head — and I screamed. "Anthony! You jerk!"

My little brother tossed back his black hood and burst out laughing. He has a high, shrill hyena laugh that makes me want to strangle him.

But I grabbed him by the shoulders instead, and shook him hard. "You little rat. You scared us to death."

That made Anthony laugh even harder.

Ivy laughed, too. "He got you this time, Mario."

"Me?" I cried. "*Me?* You were scared, too, Ivy."

"No, I wasn't," she said. "I was only pretending."

10

The sky grew even darker, and I heard the rumble of thunder in the distance.

"Let go of me," Anthony said.

I didn't realize I was still gripping his shoulders.

He stamped hard on my right foot.

"Owwww!" I uttered a cry and staggered back.

Anthony laughed again. He's a little creep. He's always following me and trying to scare me. I'd like to smash him. But as the man of the house, my job is to watch over him and take care of him as best I can.

The truth is, I can't really hate him. Mainly because he looks just like me. We both have thick, wavy black hair, round faces, dark eyes, and we're tall and kind of beefy.

"Look what I found," Anthony said. He grabbed my hand and started to pull me along the grassy path between the graves.

The wind felt wet. It shook the trees and sent the dead leaves skipping over the old tombstones.

"Look," Anthony said, pointing down.

Ivy and I stared at a deep hole in the ground. "It's an open grave," Ivy said.

I shivered again. I pulled my jacket tighter. "It's an open grave, waiting for someone," I murmured. I grabbed Anthony. "Maybe it's waiting for *you*!"

He pulled away. "Maybe it's waiting for someone named Mario," he said. His dark eyes flashed. "I dare you to jump down there."

My eyes darted over the grave. It was deep and the mud walls were black. Even in the dim light, I could see fat worms crawling over the grave floor.

Ivy laughed.

"What's so funny?" I snapped.

"Your face," she said. "You look so terrified. It's just a mud hole, Mario."

"No, it isn't," I replied. "Someone dug this for a dead person. It isn't a hole — it's a grave."

"I *knew* you couldn't do it," Anthony said. He jumped up and down, like he'd won a big victory. "I'm braver than you are! I'm braver than you are!"

Ivy turned to me. Her green eyes locked on mine. "Go ahead. Jump in," she whispered. "Don't let Anthony win."

I squinted into the grave. I watched the worms crawling in the mud at the bottom. It looked so dark and disgusting down there. But I had just met Ivy. I didn't want her to think I was a coward.

I stepped to the edge.

Should I do it? Should I jump?

Before I could decide, someone gave me a hard shove from behind.

"Hey!" I let out a scream — and went sailing into the grave.

3

"Owww." I landed hard on my elbows and knees. Pain shot down my whole body.

I struggled to climb to my feet. The strong smell of the mud floor rose to my nostrils. Wet clumps of dirt smeared my hands.

Ivy and Anthony peered down at me. I growled and shook my fist at my brother. "You pushed me — you rat! I'll get you! I'm not kidding. You'll be sorry, you jerk."

Anthony's eyes grew wide. "But ... I didn't," he stammered. "Mario — I swear. I didn't push you."

"Liar!" I screamed. "You dirty liar!" I tried to rub the mud off my hands on the legs of my jeans.

"I never touched you," Anthony insisted.

"He's telling the truth," Ivy called down. The wind gusted hard, almost drowning out her voice. She brushed her hair out of her eyes. "I was watching him, Mario. He didn't push you."

"Oh, yeah?" I snarled. "Someone shoved me down here. Who was it?"

13

Ivy laughed. "Maybe it was a ghost."

Rain started to come down. Big, heavy drops that made a *splat* sound on the muddy grave floor.

I rubbed my back. It still ached from the hard push. I don't believe in ghosts. Anthony had to be lying. He pushed me. It's the kind of thing Anthony likes to do.

Ivy was just trying to protect him.

Rain slapped the sides of the grave. "Get me out of here," I said. "It's too deep. I can't climb out by myself."

Ivy had her hands on her knees. She bent over the grave. "You can't climb up the side?"

"It's too muddy," I said. "I'd just slide right back down."

She turned to Anthony. "Come help me."

They both reached down for me. I raised my arms to them. They each grabbed a hand and tugged. I saw the dirt at the side of the grave crumble away.

"Noooo!" Ivy screamed as she started to fall.

I staggered back as they both came tumbling into the grave.

Anthony landed on his feet. His body appeared to bounce, but he kept his balance.

Ivy landed facedown in the mud.

"I don't believe this," I muttered. I grabbed Ivy by the shoulders of her sweater and helped pull her to her feet.

14

She blinked a few times, stunned. Then she grinned at me. "I wasn't expecting a mud bath today," she said. "Look at me. I'm dripping in mud. So *this* is what pigs feel like."

Cheerful. Always cheerful.

"I . . . I'm not happy right now," Anthony murmured.

"Going down into the grave was *your* idea," I said.

He shook his head. "I wanted *you* to go into the grave — not me."

The raindrops came down harder. Above us, I could hear the wind swirling through the graves.

I dug both hands into the grave wall and tried to climb. But my hands slid right back down. The mud fell off in big clumps.

Lightning crackled above us.

"We've got to get out of here," I said.

Without another word, all three of us began to scream.

"Help! Help us! Can anybody hear us? Somebody — *help!*"

4

We didn't scream for long. We knew the grave-yard was empty. We hadn't seen another person anywhere nearby. Besides, the wind was howl-ing so loudly, it drowned out our shouts.

The rain pounded down. My hair was matted to my head. I kept wiping raindrops from my eyes.

I felt cold water seep into my shoes. I gazed down and saw that deep puddles were spreading across the mud of the grave floor. Worms crawled over my feet and up my pant legs.

Ivy started to hop up and down. To keep warm, I guess.

"We can figure this out," she said. "Mario, give me a boost."

She moved to a grave wall. I cupped my hands under her shoes. And pushed.

Her hands scrabbled at the top. The dirt gave way, and she started to slide back down. But I held on. Held her steady.

I gave her another push. She dug her fingers into the mud and, with a groan, hoisted herself out of the grave. She disappeared from view for a few seconds. I heard her give a cheer.

Then she returned, peering down at Anthony and me. "Give me your hands," she said. Anthony shoved me from behind. Ivy tugged me out. Then we both pulled Anthony up.

The cold, swirling wind made me shiver. All three of us were soaked and covered with mud.

Lightning crackled again, followed by a boom of rolling thunder.

"Let's get out of here!" I shouted.

I led the way. Ducking our heads against the rain, we took a few running steps toward my house.

And then we froze.

Voices whispered all around us. Voices carried by the wind. Behind us. Ahead of us. Everywhere.

"Just the rain," I murmured. Every muscle in my body tensed. I listened to the whispers — and knew it couldn't be the wind.

I heard their words so clearly.

"Visit me . . ."

"Come to me. Visit me . . ."

"I'm soooooo lonely . . ."

Hoarse, raspy voices. Voices from the graves? The dead and buried . . . calling to us? Pleading with us?

I pressed my hands over my ears. I tried to shut them out.

But I could still hear their hoarse cries:

"Come here. Come over here . . ."

"I won't hurt you. I'm so lonely . . ."

And then I screamed in horror when a bony hand squeezed my shoulder from behind.

5

Struggling to catch my breath, I spun around. "Anthony!"

He raised both hands. "I didn't do anything."

"You liar. You grabbed me." I grasped the front of his coat and angrily pulled him toward me.

"No. I didn't touch you," he protested. "I swear." He pulled free of my grasp.

Ivy stepped between us. "He didn't grab you, Mario," she said. "Stop acting crazy and let's get home."

Acting crazy?

Was it crazy? I could still hear the voices all around.

Someone pushed me into that grave, and someone squeezed my shoulder. *Someone* . . . living or dead?

I realized my whole body was trembling.

Would I remember this day as the scariest day of my life?

The three of us began to run again. Ivy turned

at the street. "I'm going home," she cried. "This is too scary. See you later."

I watched her run toward her house on the next block. Anthony and I darted up the front steps to our house.

"We're going from a haunted graveyard to a haunted house," I muttered.

"Our new house isn't haunted," Anthony said. "It's just old."

"Old and haunted," I insisted.

I fumbled with the front doorknob. The old wooden door was stuck. It took all my strength to pull it open. We burst inside, both breathing hard, shaking off rainwater.

I was desperate to tell Mom what happened in the graveyard. But she wasn't home. She was at one of her jobs.

Anthony and I tossed our wet clothes in the laundry hamper. We dried ourselves off and pulled on clean T-shirts and jeans.

Mom had left a pot of tomato soup on the stove with instructions on how long to cook it. I found a loaf of bread and made cheese sandwiches for the two of us.

Anthony and I ate our lunch at the kitchen table. We didn't talk much. I kept seeing the deep, dark hole of the grave and the worms and the mud, and hearing the howling wind and the whispered, raspy voices. They played in my mind like a horror movie.

Anthony was probably thinking the same frightening thoughts. Neither one of us wanted to talk about any of it.

Ivy came over before lunch was over. She wore a long, black skirt and a different green sweater. She finished the tomato soup in the pot and ate the second half of my cheese sandwich.

"Graveyards can make you hungry," she said, smiling as always.

"Don't mention the graveyard," I said.

"Do you have any cookies?" she asked. She started opening cabinet drawers. She pulled out a box of graham crackers. "Oh, I love graham crackers. I could eat a whole box."

We passed around the graham crackers. "Where does your mother work?" Ivy asked.

"At the box factory downtown," I said. "She's some kind of secretary."

"My mom is a bank teller," Ivy said.

"Does she ever bring home any samples?" Anthony asked.

That made us laugh. Sometimes Anthony can be funny. When he isn't being a complete pest.

I couldn't shake off the scene in the graveyard. I couldn't think about anything else. "It . . . it was like the graveyard was *alive*," I said.

Ivy's expression turned serious. She set down the box of graham crackers. "My brother, Stan . . . He's always reading. He's a real bookworm. Stan read a book about zombies."

"Zombies?" I asked.

She nodded. "Yeah. You know. Dead people who come back to life. And all they want to do is eat human flesh."

"Yum!" Anthony said. He crunched up a cracker between his teeth. "Flesh! I love flesh!"

"Shut up," I snapped. "You don't even know what flesh is."

"Do too." I had a graham cracker in front of me on the table. He smashed it with his fist.

"You'll eat that!" I said.

"Cut it out, you two," Ivy said. "Don't you realize we might have heard zombies in the graveyard this morning? Don't you think those whispers we heard —"

"Stop!" I said. I pressed my hands over my ears.

Anthony laughed. "My big brother, Mario, is afraid of zombies! Afraid they'll want to *eat* you?" He turned and bit my arm.

"Hey! That hurt!" I gave him a hard shove.

He tossed back his head and laughed again. What a little creep.

I turned back to Ivy. "I don't believe in zombies," I said. "I don't believe in ghosts, and I don't believe in dead people whispering in graveyards."

She shrugged. "We heard something, Mario. It wasn't just the wind."

"Let's do something," I said. I was desperate to change the subject. I was scared. I mean, really scared. But I didn't want Ivy to know.

I jumped up and pushed my chair in. "Let's go to the den and play some records. My dad has a pretty good collection of jazz records." I started to lead them down the hall toward the den.

There was a stack of cartons at the end of the hall. Mom hadn't had time to unpack everything.

Ivy stopped and peered into a doorway. "Hey, you have a basement. My house doesn't have a basement. Have you been down there?"

"No," I said. "Not yet."

"Why don't we explore your basement?" Ivy said. She pulled the door all the way open. "Maybe there are some amazing treasures down there. Who owned this house before you?"

I shrugged. "Beats me. I think the house was empty for a long time. I mean, look at it." I pointed to the broken floorboards. Then I raised my eyes to the peeling paint on the walls. "It's a total wreck."

"Mario doesn't want to go in the basement," Anthony chimed in. "He's too scared."

"Shut up, Anthony," I snapped. "Why don't you go up to your room and amuse yourself?"

"Why don't you go fly a kite?"

"Come on, you two," Ivy pleaded. "Follow me." She turned and started down the basement stairs.

I didn't really want to go. That little creep Anthony was right. I was scared. Actually, I was still shaken from our cemetery adventure. But I had no choice. I had to follow Ivy.

I grabbed a flashlight from the supply closet. And I started down the wooden stairs. They were very steep and narrow, and covered with a layer of slippery dust. They creaked and groaned under our feet.

My flashlight beam swept up and down over the basement floor. The air grew cooler as we headed down. A sour odor greeted my nose.

I stopped halfway down. I realized my heart was pounding in my chest.

One thought flashed through my mind: *This house is so creepy. Are we going to find something horrible down there?*

We huddled at the bottom of the stairs. A small rectangle of light spread in front of us on the floor, light from upstairs. My flashlight beam darted over the bare basement walls.

"It stinks down here," I muttered. "And it's cold as a refrigerator."

Ivy took a few steps into the darkness. "It's a pretty big basement," she said. "And look — it's filled with junk."

I swept the light past her. I saw stacks of cardboard cartons, piles of tattered newspapers, a long rack of old-fashioned-looking clothes — long skirts and frilly blouses. Even in the dim light, I could see that the clothes were moth-eaten and stained.

Ivy walked over to the clothes. Anthony and I followed her. Anthony pulled an old magazine off a pile. It crumbled in his hands. "That's ancient," he said.

25

"Someone moved out of this house a long time ago," Ivy said, "and just left all this stuff down here. I wonder why."

I swept the beam of light around in a circle. "It would take *weeks* to clean out this place," I said.

Ivy bent down and lifted some boxes from a large straw basket. "Board games," she said. "Old board games. Maybe some of these are still fun to play."

But then she made a disgusted face and let them fall back into the basket. "Ooh, they're covered in mold. And they all smell so terrible."

I squeezed my nose. "This whole basement smells like rotten meat," I said. "Why does it stink so bad?"

"Maybe because of this dead mouse," Anthony said. I swung the light beam around. And I watched Anthony pick up a headless, half-decayed mouse by the tail.

"Drop it!" I cried. "Are you *crazy*?"

Holding the tail in two fingers, he swung it in front of him. An evil grin spread over his face. "Here — catch!" he called. He heaved the dead mouse at me.

I tried to dodge away. But it smacked me in the chest.

I staggered back. The flashlight fell out of my hand and clattered onto the cement floor.

Anthony laughed his shrill hyena laugh.

And then I went bonkers. I grabbed the flashlight. And with a furious growl, I went charging at Anthony.

He probably thought I was going to hit him with the flashlight. But I would never do anything like that to my kid brother. Instead, I lowered my shoulder — and butted him backward with all my strength.

"Noooo!" He let out a cry as he lost his balance. He slammed hard into a stack of cartons. The big boxes toppled from side to side — and then came crashing down.

I gasped as a huge box landed on Anthony, flattening him to the floor. One arm poked out from under the carton. He didn't move. He didn't make a sound.

I froze in terror, staring at him flat on his back under the box.

Ivy ran over to him and dropped to her knees beside him. "You *crushed* him!" she screamed. "Mario — you crushed your brother!"

"Noooo! Oh, no!"

A cry escaped my throat. I dove beside Ivy and stared down at my brother, at the arm sticking out so lifelessly from under the huge box.

And then I heard Anthony giggle.

Ivy and I blinked at each other. I raised both hands and gave the carton a push.

It practically flew off Anthony. It was light as a feather.

Anthony raised his head and grinned. "Were you scared?" He laughed again and scrambled to his feet before I could punch him.

My heart was still pounding. "You scared Ivy and me to death, you creep."

That made him laugh harder.

I picked up the carton. It was empty. It couldn't crush an ant.

"Can we go upstairs now?" I asked Ivy.

She wasn't looking at me. She was squinting down at the floor. "What is that?" She pointed.

I swept the flashlight beam down to where she pointed. It took me a few seconds to focus my eyes. "It seems to be some kind of handle," I said.

Ivy squatted down to examine it more closely. "A handle in the floor?"

Anthony and I joined her. I aimed the circle of light at it. "A trapdoor," I said. "See? It's a trapdoor in the floor. You pull up the handle and —"

Anthony dove across me and grabbed the handle. "Let's see what's down there."

"No, wait —" I tried to pull him back. "Maybe we don't want to —"

Too late. Anthony tugged and the trapdoor slid open. He pulled it all the way up until it stood on its own.

We stared into the square opening. I could see a rope ladder that led down into total darkness.

"How weird," Ivy murmured. "It's a basement under the basement."

"Anthony, we don't know what's down there," I said.

Ivy leaned over the opening. "Can't see a thing from up here."

"Let's go," Anthony said. He lowered himself into the opening and grabbed the rope ladder with both hands.

"Anthony, no — !" I shouted.

But when does he ever listen to me?

I tried to pull him away. But he was already making his way down the ladder. I could only see his head and shoulders. "Come on. Follow the leader!" he cried.

He disappeared from view.

I turned to Ivy. "Are we going down there?"

"It's an adventure," she said. "How can you resist a secret room under the basement?"

"Easy," I said. I peered into the hole. "Hey, Anthony?" I called down. My voice echoed from somewhere down there. "Anthony?"

I couldn't see him at all. I swung the flashlight and aimed it into the hole. "Anthony, where are you? Hey, I can't see you. Where are you? Anthony — come back up here!"

I darted the flashlight all around. No sign of him. My heart started to pound. I suddenly felt cold all over.

"Anthony?"

And then I heard a shrill, terrified scream from far below: "Help! It's *got* me! It's *got* me!"

I turned to Ivy and rolled my eyes. "How many times is he going to pull this joke?" I said.

She nodded. "I don't believe him, either. He's a complete fake."

"Anthony, you're not fooling us," I shouted down into the opening. "Not for a second. Come back up and stop trying to scare us."

Silence.

Ivy leaned into the hole and cupped her hands around her mouth and shouted. "Anthony? You're not funny, Anthony. Come back where we can see you."

Silence.

"Anthony?" I called, my voice growing shrill. "Anthony? Hey — Anthony?"

Ivy and I waited, our eyes focused on the darkness below. My heart began to pound. The silence rang in my ears.

Finally, Anthony stepped into the light. He gazed up at us, a big grin on his face. "I didn't scare you? Are you lying?"

"We're not lying," I said. "You tried it once too often. Now get back up here."

"No. You come down," he insisted. "It's kind of strange down here."

"Strange?" Ivy called. "What do you mean?"

Anthony motioned us down. "Come here. You'll see."

Ivy shrugged. She moved into the opening and grabbed both sides of the rope ladder. I watched her lower herself down a rung at a time.

I had a bad feeling about this. But, of course, I had a bad feeling about *everything* in this old house. I kept asking myself, why would there be a basement under the basement? Did the past owner of this house have something he needed to hide?

I grabbed the rope ladder. My feet fumbled for the rungs. I'd never climbed on a rope ladder. And it was shakier and more difficult than I imagined — especially while gripping a flashlight in one hand.

But I made it to the bottom, let go of the ladder, took a few steps back, and glanced around.

My eyes followed the light of my flashlight. "There's nothing down here," I said. "It's completely empty. Just walls and a dirt floor."

Ivy squinted at my brother. "Anthony, why did you think it's so interesting?"

He pointed. "Look."

I swung the light around. The bare walls gave way to a dark, narrow passage. It seemed to go on forever. "A . . . tunnel," I murmured.

"Yes. This isn't a room," Anthony said. "It's a tunnel."

Ivy squinted into the light. "A long tunnel under your house. But where does it lead?"

"Let's follow it," Anthony said. He started to trot into the dark passage.

"Wait," I said. "Let's think about this."

"Maybe it leads to some fantastic caves," he said. "Maybe it leads to the ocean!"

Ivy and I laughed. "That would be a very long tunnel," she said. "Franklin Village is miles and miles from any ocean."

I thought hard. I gazed up at the trapdoor opening high above us. And then I followed the floor of the tunnel. "I think I know where the tunnel leads," I said in a whisper.

"Where?" Ivy asked.

"To the graveyard."

9

Anthony laughed. "How do *you* know?"

"Yes. How do you know that?" Ivy said. "You're just guessing, Mario."

I nodded. "Right. I'm guessing. But look at it. It leads toward the street. And what is across the street? The graveyard."

Anthony grinned at Ivy. "Now we *have* to follow it — just to prove Mario wrong." He took off, trotting into the darkness of the narrow tunnel.

"No. Wait —" I called.

But Ivy followed him. I had no choice. "Wait up."

My light beam swept from side to side as I kept it ahead of us. The tunnel was so low, we had to duck our heads. The walls and floor were dirt. Our shoes kicked up dust as we ran.

"I . . . can't believe we're doing this," I said, breathing hard. "If Mom knew about this, she'd *kill* us."

"We're just exploring," Ivy said. "What is the big deal?"

"Maybe there's pirate treasure hidden at the end," Anthony said.

"We're under the street now," I said. "I just know it." I wiped sweat off my forehead with the back of my hand. The deeper we moved into the tunnel, the warmer the air became. The smell of the dirt started to choke me.

The tunnel curved a little to the left. I kept the light beam on the floor ahead of us. My loud breaths echoed off the dirt walls.

All three of us stopped when we heard the sounds.

I tried to swallow but my mouth was too dry. Anthony and Ivy were breathing hard, too. We had our eyes straight ahead, listening hard.

Were those animal growls?

I heard the scrape of footsteps on the dirt.

I aimed the light straight ahead. But I couldn't see anything in the deep darkness.

I gasped when I heard a loud groan. And then a cough.

"We . . . we're not alone down here," I stammered. My hand shook. I almost dropped the flashlight.

The scraping footsteps came closer.

"L-let's get out of here," I whispered.

But all three of us were frozen to the spot. Our mouths open. Breathing hard in the dirt-choked air. Listening.

36

We all cried out as the hunched figures staggered into view. Were they people? They walked on two legs. But they grunted and growled like animals.

I swept the light from face to face — and every muscle in my body tightened in horror.

Their faces were twisted and ugly. Some had missing eyes. Some had big patches of skin rotted away, the gray skull showing through. Their clothes were tattered and in filthy shreds. Their feet were bare and all bone. Skeletal feet. No skin at all.

"Zombies," Ivy whispered. She grabbed my arm. "Dead people ... walking. From the graveyard."

Grunting, they shuffled toward us. They were only a few feet from us, staggering closer.

Frightening thoughts flew through my mind. *This tunnel must be their hiding place. Where they can travel safely without being seen. But why are they moving toward us now? Because they're* hungry?

Anthony seemed paralyzed by the terrifying sight. I squeezed his shoulder hard and tugged. "Let's go. *Move!*"

Ivy was already running hard, kicking up dirt as she raced back to the trapdoor. Anthony and I ran side by side, leaning forward as we moved, as if that would help us get there sooner.

The light from my flashlight twisted and jerked, like flashes of lightning in front of us. Over my hard, heavy breaths, I could hear the shuffling, bony feet of the zombies. Hear their hungry grunts, their animal groans.

Were they catching up? I didn't dare turn around to see.

Our pounding shoes kicked up dirt. A gust of wind through the tunnel made it swirl around us. I choked on it. My eyes were burning and dripping tears.

Ivy stopped and covered her face, coughing from the dirt.

I pulled her toward the trapdoor. "Don't stop. We're almost there."

Our shoes pounded the tunnel floor. Finally, I could see a square of light above us.

"The trapdoor," I said, my voice a hoarse whisper. "Hurry."

My heart thudding in my chest, I grabbed the sides of the rope ladder. The ladder swung back and forth. But my foot found the bottom rung. I gripped the sides tightly and began to pull myself up to safety.

"Nooooo!"

A scream escaped my throat as the ladder broke off. It came loose at the top.

I was still screaming as I hit the floor hard, and the ladder crumpled down on top of me.

10

On my back on the floor, I thrashed my arms and legs, trying to untangle myself from the fallen ladder. Ivy and Anthony grabbed the ropes and tossed the thing aside.

I jumped to my feet, gasping for breath. And stared up at the opening so far above our heads. Safety up there. And no way to get there.

No way to escape the grunting, decayed bodies shuffling and staggering toward us.

"Get back! Stay away!" Anthony screamed at them.

But they just kept coming. Could they even hear us? I squinted into the dim light. Most of them had lost their ears.

They'd lost whole patches of skin on their heads. Cheeks missing. Gray bone poking out from stretched, green skin. They grinned as they marched forward, toothless, lipless grins.

The rancid odor of their decaying bodies poured over us. I gagged, struggling not to vomit.

"Wh-what do we do?" Ivy asked in a tiny, trembling voice.

I gazed up at the trapdoor. It seemed a mile above our heads.

We had nowhere to run. No way to escape.

I couldn't answer Ivy. I could only stand there, my whole body shaking.

Could only stand there and watch as the hideous figures, their toothless mouths bobbing up and down, surrounded us, grunting with excitement.

A tall, hunched guy with half his face rotted away, one eye hanging from its socket, reached a bony hand forward — and grabbed me by the throat.

I heard Ivy and Anthony scream in horror.

A sharp cry escaped my mouth as the hideous, undead creature pulled me to him. And lowered his head to my shoulder to feed on my flesh.

11

"No, please. No — please!"

He ignored my choked cries. My knees sagged. My whole body went limp.

I shut my eyes and prepared for the pain. He lifted me off the floor. Held me by the throat. His rotted brown teeth clicked several times and lowered to my shoulder.

"Hey!" I uttered a confused cry as the creature tossed me away.

He heaved me to the tunnel wall. My back slid down the dirt wall until I was sitting on the floor. Dazed and terrified, I gazed up at the tall, undead creature. He had turned away from me.

He doesn't want to feed on me. What does *he want to do?*

Ivy and Anthony pressed their backs against the wall. Ivy covered her face with her hands. Anthony stood frozen, his eyes bulging, his shoulders trembling.

The tall zombie bent over with a groan. His bony hands scrabbled on the floor. They grasped the fallen rope ladder.

He wants to climb out of the tunnel, I realized.

The zombie turned himself around, his dangling eyeball swinging in the air. Then he raised the ladder toward the square opening above. Two other zombies, their faces green with mold, their clothes in worm-eaten tatters, moved to help him.

In the dim light, I saw three or four more undead creatures. They were hanging back in the shadows, grunting softly as they watched.

The tall zombie climbed on another zombie's back. He stretched his arms to hang the ladder back up. It took a long time because his hands fumbled and shook, and he kept dropping it back to the floor.

As I watched helplessly, my mind whirred with frightening thoughts. This tunnel stretched from their graves. The zombies used the tunnel to be safe, safe from humans who would hunt them down.

But now they were climbing into the world of the living.

I watched helplessly as the creature hung the ladder back in place. And the zombies were climbing, climbing up to my basement. *Into my house.*

And that's when I heard a sound that sent a shock of fear down my body. My mother's voice. My mother, calling from the hall upstairs. "Mario? Anthony? Where are you? Are you in the basement?"

Panic made my throat tighten until I choked.

The zombies will see her.

Will the zombies eat her first?

"Mom!" I screamed. "Get out of the house! Run! Get out of the house — *now!*"

12

I had to do something. The first zombie was nearly to the top of the ladder, about to climb into my basement.

"Mom!" I screamed. "Can you hear me? Run! Get out of the house!"

"Mario, is that you?" she called from upstairs. "What are you saying? I can't hear you."

I pushed myself off the wall. I knew I had to act. I couldn't let these deadly creatures devour my mother.

I took a deep breath — and leaped at the zombie on the ladder. I grabbed him around the waist — and heaved him to the floor.

He groaned and collapsed against the wall. I could hear his bones cracking. His dangling eyeball swung in front of his head.

My fear gave me strength I didn't know I had. With a loud cry, I hoisted up another zombie — and threw him into the tunnel. He crashed into the wall, and his head split open.

I swung around to face the rest of the zombies. They stepped back, chattering, preparing another attack.

I didn't give them the chance. I grabbed the sides of the rope ladder and pulled myself up to the basement. Anthony came climbing right behind me.

When we were both safely in the basement, we slammed the trapdoor shut behind us.

Over my panting breaths and the drumbeats of my heart, I could still hear the chattering of the ugly creatures down below.

I spun away from them and ran up the basement steps, taking them two at a time.

"Mom!" I gasped, racing down the hall to the kitchen. "Mom! Zombies! Under the house! There are zombies under our house!"

She turned slowly from the kitchen sink. "I know," she said.

13

"Huh?" I leaned on the counter, struggling to catch my breath.

Anthony dropped onto a tall kitchen stool. I could see he was still shaking in fear.

"You — you know about the zombies?" I stammered.

Mom squeezed the water out of a sponge and tossed it in the sink. She is dark, like Anthony and me, with wavy black hair and olive eyes. Mom is short and very thin. I'm twelve and I'm almost as tall as she is.

She used to be the cheerful one in the family. But since Dad went away to the war, she doesn't smile as much as she used to. I guess working two jobs makes her too tired to be her old enthusiastic self.

She sighed. "I heard the stories about this house. But they sounded so crazy."

"Huh? What do you mean?" I asked.

"The real estate agent warned me," Mom said. "She said 324 North Ardmore was a house of the dead. Who could believe that? Besides, I had no choice. It was all I could afford."

I wiped sweat off my forehead with the back of my hand. "You mean, you knew when you bought this house —"

Mom bit her bottom lip. Her hands were trembling. "Where did you see them? Are they locked up?"

"I'll show you," I said. I turned to my brother. "Do you want to stay up here?"

He shook his head. "No. I'll come, too."

"They're in the basement?" Mom asked.

"They're *under* the basement," I said. I led the way. Our shoes clunked loudly on the wooden basement steps.

I led Mom to the trapdoor in the floor. It was silent in the basement and silent down below. Mom's hands were squeezed into tight fists.

She bent down and lifted the trapdoor.

We all screamed as a creature roared up from below.

Ivy!

Ivy. But her eyes were blank. Her green sweater was in shreds. Her hair fell in wet tangles. And her nose . . . her cute, pointed elf nose — it was *gone*! Just a hole in her face.

She gaped at me with those dead, dead eyes. *"Mario . . ."* she groaned.

"Ivy! Oh, noooo!" I wailed. "We forgot you! We forgot you. We left you down there! What did they *do* to you?"

She growled at me, an animal growl from deep in her throat. *"I'll get you, Mario. You'll never escape me.* Never!"

PART TWO

TODAY

14

The buildings were dark. The long, narrow street was empty. The wind whistled through the town, one shrill, steady note that hurt my ears.

In the distance, I saw a black cat scuttle across the street. It vanished into an alley behind a darkened store. A trash can rolled on its side, pushed by the streaming wind.

I stepped off the curb. My eyes darted from side to side. I knew the emptiness wasn't real. I knew the silence wouldn't last.

I was being watched.

I walked slowly down the middle of the street. I glanced into parked cars. I kept turning my head and looking behind me. I could feel the tension in my chest, feel it in my tightened fists.

The rushing wind blew dead leaves at my feet. I jumped over them. I kept my eyes ahead of me.

Another trash can rolled silently down the empty sidewalk. I crossed into the next block, dark stores stretching on both sides. I stared into the narrow spaces between the buildings. Watching. Waiting. Alert.

Ready.

At least, I *thought* I was ready.

But when the creature attacked, I cried out in surprise.

He was twice my size, hulking and huge, with a shadow that covered me in heavy darkness. His eyes bulged like glassy billiard balls. His chin had been torn away. Only his long, top teeth remained, poking down over a lipless gap of a mouth.

The creature's stringy hair hung limply at the sides of his pale green face. I could see fat black insects trapped in the tangles.

He raised huge fists as he leaped on me, his hands swollen like overripe melons. He uttered a low animal grunt and tried to wrap me up in his enormous arms, pull me into the decayed flesh of his belly.

"No way, zombie!" I screamed. "No way!"

I ducked my head under his enormous chest — and shot forward. A powerful head-butt that made him grunt. He doubled over, drool pouring down his half-missing face.

I smashed both fists into his belly, which collapsed like a deflating balloon. He grunted again and toppled backward onto the sidewalk.

Squeezing my fists, I stepped over him. I took two more steps and saw a pack of zombies scramble out from between the buildings. They glanced up and down the street. It didn't take them long to see me.

Groaning, rubbing their bellies through their tattered clothes, they staggered toward me. Their bulging eyes revealed their hunger. They bleated like sheep as they came at me.

I could feel them tugging at my mind. . . . Some kind of mind control power. Holding me in place . . . trying to keep me helpless, unable to move.

I shut my eyes — and tried the head-butting trick again. Against a frail-looking zombie, thin as a potato chip. But this time, I missed his chest, my head hitting air.

Two other creatures leaped on my back. I swung my arms and struggled to keep my feet. But they were surprisingly strong.

They had me on my back.

And then they all swarmed at once.

Bony hands pawed at me. The grunts and groans rang in my ears.

I screamed as their sharp fingers punctured my chest — and ripped it open.

I kept screaming as they lowered their ugly heads and began to feed.

15

"I died again!" I screamed.

My friend Alec Schwartzman shook his head. "Bad news, Kenny. You should have run. You don't have the weapons to fight them."

I slammed the controller on the floor. "I'm never going to get beyond Level One."

Alec and I were playing the new version of *The Walking Zombies*.

"You can probably fight them one at a time," he said. "But when a pack of them appears, you have to turn and go down another street."

Alec had a lot of advice. But he was just as bad at the game as I was.

We'd been playing for an hour, and I still hadn't stayed alive to the other end of town. That's kind of annoying, right?

I turned to my twin sister, Tricia, and snapped at her. "Why are you staring at us? Go away. You're a jinx."

I *knew* why Tricia was hanging around. She has a major league crush on Alec.

"I'm not a jinx," she said, shoving me into the couch. "You're just a klutz, Kenny."

Alec laughed at that. I don't know why. Maybe he has a crush on Tricia.

My name is Kenny Manzetti. Tricia and I are twelve. But we look older than our age. I mean, Alec is twelve, too. But he looks like a little, red-haired kid next to us.

For one thing, Tricia and I are taller than most kids our age. And we have kind of serious faces — dark eyes, straight dark hair.

Mom says we're "old souls." I don't really know what that's supposed to mean. It's not like we act much like adults. Tricia and I like to hang out with kids and have fun.

At least, we did at our old school. We haven't met too many kids to hang out with at our new school. In fact, Alec is the only friend I've made here in Franklin Village.

If you want to know the truth, Tricia and I are trying to be good sports. But we really don't like our new house. For one thing, I *hate* living across the street from a graveyard. It gives me a lot of bad dreams. Seriously.

Alec elbowed me. "Boot the game up. Let's try again."

We were sitting side by side on the den floor in

front of the TV. Tricia hunched on the edge of the couch behind us. "I don't get the whole zombie thing," she said.

"Then why don't you go away?" I asked.

"I mean, why is everyone at school obsessed with zombies?" she kept on. "Is it because of that TV show your game is based on? *The Walking Zombies*?"

"Like duh," I said.

"It's an awesome show," Alec said. "Are you watching season three?"

"I'm only up to season two," I said. "Don't tell me what happens in the next season."

Tricia laughed. "What happens in the next season? I'll tell you. A bunch of zombies stagger around eating people. Zombies are so way boring."

"Why don't you go up to your room and play with your American Girl dolls?" I said. "You're annoying."

She bonked the top of my head. "I don't play with dolls, dumb head. I collect them. My collection is worth a lot of money."

Alec reached into his jeans pocket and pulled out a pack of Zombie Goop Loops. He popped one in his mouth, then offered them to Tricia and me. Naturally, she said, "Bleh. How disgusting."

She's wrong. It's a pretty good candy. Comes in a lot of flavors. All the kids at our new school are into them.

I started the game again.

"Do you want to change the difficulty level?" Alec asked. "I think there's a Baby level."

"Haha," I said. "How funny are you?"

I saw movement outside the living room window. I squinted across the street. I saw two people in dark raincoats walking through the graveyard. Every once in a while, they stopped to read a gravestone.

Did I mention that I don't like graveyards?

I'm not superstitious or anything. I don't believe zombies can rise up from their graves and go after people. I just think it's creepy to have all those dead people lying there across the street from you.

My dad told me about this superstition. He said a lot of people hold their breath till they get past a graveyard. But I can't do that. I'd have to hold my breath from morning till night!

The dark, empty town appeared on the screen. Alec took the controller and prepared to face the zombies.

But he turned away from the screen and gasped as a tall, frail figure floated into the living room. Wide-eyed, staggering, he came toward us, his pale eyes darting from Alec to me.

Alec dropped the controller. "A . . . a zombie!" he cried.

16

The pale old man laughed. His laugh came out dry, like a cough. "A zombie? That's what I *feel* like these days!" he exclaimed.

Alec was still gazing openmouthed at him.

"Alec, this is my grandfather," I said. "Everyone calls him Grandpa Mo."

Alec swallowed and seemed to go back to normal. "Hi," he said. He gave Grandpa Mo a little wave.

My grandfather waved back. He made his way slowly to the couch and dropped down next to Tricia. He has a bad limp. His right knee is totally worn-out. But he refuses to use a cane.

He's not very strong, and he coughs a lot. He says everything on his body hurts, even his hair. He has a full head of thick, wavy white hair, which he carefully brushes. Sometimes he stands at the mirror for more than ten minutes.

His skin is tight on his narrow face, and almost

as white as his hair. His eyes are so pale, sometimes they look entirely white, no pupils at all.

Don't get the wrong idea. He's a tough old dude.

Tricia and I haven't seen him since we were five. It's kind of a long story.

I'll try to make it short. He's my dad's dad, see. But somehow, my parents lost track of him. No one saw him or heard from him for a lot of years. The old guy just disappeared.

But then, here he was, back in his house. This is Grandpa Mo's house. Mom and Dad thought he was too old and sick to live alone. So we all moved into his house in Franklin Village.

Mom teaches third grade at the elementary school. And Dad is an investment manager at the bank in the next town.

And now I think you know everything about us. Oh. Except for one other thing about Grandpa Mo: He loves to tell zombie stories.

Sometimes he says they are true. Sometimes he says he dreams them. I know he makes them all up. But I can't tell if he believes them or not.

"Put away the game, boys, and I'll tell you a true story," he said. His voice is soft and sometimes hard to hear. His hand tapped a rhythm on the arm of the couch.

Alec set the controller on the floor, and we turned to face Grandpa Mo. Tricia rolled her eyes, so only I could see. She doesn't like Grandpa

Mo's stories. She thinks anything about zombies is dumb.

"Many years ago, there was a powerful storm in Franklin Village," Grandpa Mo started. "There were lightning attacks everywhere. I mean, not your normal lightning. It didn't crackle — it boomed like thunder.

"The lightning snapped trees in half and darted over the lawns like some kind of living creature. It started fires all over town. It smashed and crashed and exploded like the blast of a hundred bombs."

I squinted at Grandpa Mo. "This is really true? Were you there?"

"It doesn't matter," he said. "If I was there, I don't remember. It's hard to remember things when you're old. But I know it's true."

Tricia laughed. "You make up *all* your true stories — don't you, Grandpa Mo?"

The old man shook his head. He patted Tricia on the shoulder. But he didn't answer her. He continued his story:

"The lightning was so powerful, it woke the dead. In the cemetery right across the street from this house. Dead people, sleeping soundly in their graves, were roused by the attacking currents, the bolts of energy.

"Awakened, they climbed out of their graves. They began to walk in the storm. At first, they huddled together, confused and frightened. But then they began to feel a hunger, an overwhelming hunger. They knew they had no choice. In order to survive in this new undead state, they had to *eat the living*."

Tricia edged to the far end of the couch. "Eww. Is this going to get gross?"

Grandpa Mo shrugged his slender shoulders. "Gross? No. I think it gets frightening. Because it happened right across the street."

"Your stories are just like the TV show," Alec said. "You know. *The Walking Zombies*?"

Grandpa Mo scratched the pale, dry skin on the side of his face. "This is real. This isn't TV."

He struggled to his feet. It took him a few seconds to catch his balance. "It's my nap time," he said. "You three keep your eyes and ears open — you hear?" He limped stiffly out of the room.

Alec had a blank look on his freckled face. I could see he was thinking hard.

I laughed. "You believed Grandpa Mo's story — didn't you?" I said.

He nodded. "Yeah. I don't think he was kidding, Kenny. I think the story was true."

I knew Alec believed in all kinds of monsters and ghosts and paranormal stuff. He says there wouldn't be so many stories about vampires and zombies and other weird creatures if they didn't really exist.

I think that's kind of dumb. But he's my only friend in this new town, and he's a good guy. So I keep myself from telling him that believing in ghosts and vampires is like believing in the Tooth Fairy.

"Grandpa Mo is always telling zombie stories," I said. "He likes to make them up. He says sometimes he dreams them. But I don't think —"

Tricia bumped me with her knees as she jumped off the couch. She crossed to the living room window. "I saw a big truck outside," she said.

She pulled the curtain aside. "Hey, check it out. It's a moving van. People are moving into the house next door."

Her eyes went wide. "Oh. Wait," she said, peering out the window. "Oh, wow. Oh, wow. They're not people — they're . . . *monsters*!"

17

"Huh?" I jumped to my feet.

Alec grabbed my arm and used me to pull himself up. We both went stumbling to the window.

Tricia stepped back and laughed. "You two idiots will believe anything."

I felt my face grow hot. I was embarrassed. How could I fall for her stupid joke?

All this zombie talk was messing with my mind.

I stepped up beside Tricia and Alec. They had pushed the curtain aside and were staring over at the next house. I bumped Tricia out of the way. "I owe you one," I said.

Movers in gray uniforms were lowering furniture and big cartons off the back of a yellow-and-red van parked in the neighbors' driveway. We watched a long blue couch come off the truck. Two big men with shaved heads and tattoos around their necks struggled to balance it between them.

"I wonder who your new neighbors will be," Alec said.

"I hope there's a girl my age," Tricia said. "It's so hard to meet friends when you move to a new school so far away from home. Everyone already knows everyone."

"Hey, that's why we're having the Halloween party," I said. "To meet new kids?"

Tricia turned to me. "Yeah. What *about* the party? You two said you'd help me plan it. So, let's hear it. Where are the plans?"

"I think it should be a zombie party," Alec said. "Everyone comes dressed as a zombie."

Tricia rolled her eyes. "Of *course* you do," she said sarcastically. "Can we forget you said that and talk seriously about this party? Halloween is almost here, you know."

"Well, this is the perfect place for a spooky Halloween party," I said. I glanced around at the gray walls, the heavy, old furniture, the ragged, stained carpet. "It won't be hard to make it look like a haunted house."

Next door, the movers were carrying a long bookshelf into the house. It was a cool October day, but they were red-faced and sweating.

"Maybe we should have the party in the basement," Tricia said. "You know. Make it *really* scary."

"Awesome," I said. "We'll keep the lights off. Maybe only have candles. And hang a lot of cobwebs and creepy stuff from the ceiling."

"Nice," Alec chimed in. "But I still think

everyone should come as zombies. You could have prizes. Like, Most Disgusting Face, or Best Dried Blood, or Most Undead Looking."

"Maybe," Tricia said. "Let's think about it."

I could see she was starting to warm up to the idea. "Maybe I could be a zombie bride," she said. "You know. Wear a long white dress, all stained and ripped. Maybe a skeleton mask under my veil . . ."

"Sweet," Alec said. "Hey, where are your neighbors? Are they in the house? I haven't seen anyone over there. Just the movers."

We watched the guys carry stacks of cartons off the moving van.

"Maybe they're coming later," I said.

Tricia stepped back from the window. "This is getting kind of boring," she said.

"Wait. Look —" I cried. I squinted to focus my eyes on the back of the truck. "Look what they're carrying into the house."

Tricia pushed back between Alec and me. "Oh, wow," she murmured.

We watched them carefully lower a dark wooden coffin to the driveway.

"I . . . don't believe it," I murmured.

We didn't move. We watched the men go back into the truck. After a few seconds, they slid another coffin out. And then a third.

Three coffins going into the house next door.

18

I watched the third coffin disappear through the front door. My brain was spinning. "Who has coffins in their house?" I said.

Alec scrunched up his face. "Dead people?"

Tricia shook her head. "I really don't think there are dead people in those coffins. I mean, why would anyone —"

She stopped as Grandpa Mo lumbered back into the room. "Couldn't sleep," he said. "The whistling in my ears keeps me awake."

He swept back his white hair with one hand. "What are you looking at? You spying on someone?"

"The neighbors," I said. "The house next door. They're moving in. But . . ."

Tricia finished my sentence for me. "The movers just carried three coffins into the house."

Grandpa Mo's mouth dropped open. He staggered back a step. "Coffins?"

I nodded. "Yeah. Three of them. Weird, huh?"

"It's not as weird as you might imagine, Kenny," the old man said. He made his way to the window. Alec pulled the curtain a little wider.

Grandpa Mo stared out at the moving van. The workers were closing the back of the truck. "They seem to be finished," he said.

"But we didn't see the neighbors," I said. "Only the movers."

Grandpa Mo squeezed my shoulder. He continued to peer out the window. "That's the best way for zombies to travel," he said. "No one can see them inside a coffin."

Tricia groaned. "Oh, come on. Give us a break," she said. "You're not going to start another zombie story — are you?"

Grandpa Mo frowned at her. "You saw the coffins, didn't you?"

"Sure," Tricia said, "but there can't be any dead people in those coffins."

Alec scratched his red hair. He turned to Tricia. "Kenny is right. Who has coffins in their house?" he demanded. "Normal people? No way. Normal people don't keep coffins in their house. Your grandfather may be right. This is totally sick."

"*You're* totally sick," Tricia snapped.

I turned and saw that Grandpa Mo was trembling. I jumped up and helped him to the couch. He hugged his slender chest for a long moment.

When he finally looked up, his face was even paler than usual.

"A family of zombies has moved next door," he said in a low, shaky voice. "When they come out of those coffins . . . they'll be hungry."

19

Tricia sat down beside Grandpa Mo. She took his hand and squeezed it. "Grandpa Mo, you're letting your own stories scare you," she said. "You know those stories aren't real. Don't let them confuse you."

He didn't seem to hear her. He stared blankly across the room. "This is just what I was afraid of," he said, barely above a whisper. "I knew this day would come."

I felt bad for Grandpa Mo. I didn't like seeing him so scared. His zombie stories were scary and fun. But he seemed to believe them.

Alec was still on his knees, gazing out the window. "Hey, Kenny — check it out," he called.

I hurried over to him. "What's up?"

Alec pointed. "I saw someone move in that side window over there. They must have climbed out of their coffin."

Tricia laughed. "Did the person you see have just a skull instead of a face? Like you?"

Alec rolled his eyes. "What if he did? You wouldn't be laughing then."

I squinted across the yard into the side window. It was dark now. I didn't see anyone.

Grandpa Mo cleared his throat. He sat up straight. "Listen to me now," he said. "Here's what you have to do."

His eyes darted from Alec to me. "All three of you," he said. "Go over there."

"Huh?" I uttered. "Go over there?"

Grandpa Mo nodded. "Go next door. Say you came to say hi and welcome them to the neighborhood. Maybe they'll invite you in. Then, see what you can see."

Alec started shaking his head. "Go over there? I don't think so."

I didn't want to go, either. But I didn't like seeing my grandfather so terrified. If we could prove the new neighbors *weren't* zombies, we could stop him from shaking. And stop him from worrying.

Tricia was already on her feet. "Why do all three of you look so scared?" she demanded. "You're all zombie crazy. Get over it."

She opened the front door and stepped out. Alec and I scrambled to follow her.

The sun was low in the sky. I shielded my eyes with one hand and started across the front lawn to the house next door. The movers were just pulling away. The driver waved to me as they pulled down the driveway.

Across the street, the graveyard sat empty and silent. Some crows rested on a low tree branch, peering down at the rows of tombstones.

We crossed the driveway and walked up to the front stoop. "Kenny, Alec — stop looking like that," Tricia scolded. "Smile, okay? There's nothing to be afraid of."

We followed her up the steps to the front stoop — and I knocked on the front door.

20

A sudden gust of wind made the brown leaves skip and dance across the front yard. In the graveyard, I saw the bare trees tremble.

I heard someone moving around inside the house. But no one answered the door.

"L-let's go," Alec stammered. "I . . . really don't like this."

Tricia stomped on his foot.

Alec cried out. "Why'd you do that?"

"That was a reality check," she said. "There aren't any zombies in this house."

I knew Tricia had a crush on Alec. But she had a strange way of showing it. I think she really *was* totally fed up with all the zombie talk.

Finally, I heard the lock click on the other side of the front door. The door pulled open slowly.

A boy stuck his head out. He had thick brown hair that fell down his forehead. He had olive-green eyes. His face was pale.

"Hi," he said. He studied the three of us. Then he pulled the door open a little bit more and stepped out on the front stoop.

We backed up to make room for him. He was very thin and shorter than Tricia and me. He wore a black sweatshirt pulled down over thin-legged black jeans. He didn't smile. His face was pretty much a blank.

"Tricia and I live next door," I said, pointing to Grandpa Mo's house. "I'm Kenny. And this is my friend Alec."

The kid nodded. I figured he was about our age. "Hi," he said again.

"We saw the moving truck," Alec told him. "But we didn't see anyone from your family."

"We . . . came earlier," he said. "My name is Trevor." His eyes went to the graveyard. "You ever go over there?"

"Sometimes," Tricia answered. "It's kind of interesting. Some of the gravestones are really old."

"It's a little creepy living across from a grave-yard," I said.

"Not really," Trevor replied.

Weird answer.

I struggled to see inside the house. But the door was only open a crack, and Trevor was blocking my view.

"We just moved in, too," I said. "That's my grandfather's house."

Trevor nodded but he didn't say anything.

This was getting awkward.

I began to think he was really shy. He was so pale and quiet. He had his hands jammed into his jeans pockets.

"Are you going to go to our school?" Tricia asked. "Franklin Village Middle School?"

He shook his head. "No. My parents said I'm going to go to a private school."

"Where?" Alec asked.

Trevor shrugged. "Beats me."

I peered over his head. I could see the living room behind him. I almost lost it when I saw the three coffins. They were lined up in the middle of the living room!

Did the lid on the middle coffin move?

No. I'm seeing things.

I lowered my gaze and saw Trevor watching me. He knew that I was staring into his house.

"I've got to help my parents unpack," he said. He backed into the house, blocking my view.

"We just wanted to say hi," Tricia said.

"Thanks," Trevor replied. "See you."

He slipped inside and closed the door quietly behind him. I heard the lock click on the other side of the door.

"Totally weird," Alec whispered. "And awkward, huh?"

The three of us didn't move. We stood there blinking and thinking hard. And . . .

And . . .

Then I heard a long, low moan inside the house. And a woman's voice. A hoarse, raspy voice. I could hear her clearly through the door.

She said: "Keep unpacking, Trevor. Don't worry. We'll find some food soon."

21

I hopped off the stoop. I wanted to get away from there. I could still hear the woman's voice in my ears. So hoarse and breathy.

I trotted back to Grandpa Mo's house with Alec and Tricia close behind. We all had the same questions on our mind: Was Trevor just a pale, shy kid? Or was Grandpa Mo right? Was he someone we should be afraid of?

My grandfather was waiting for us in the living room. He hadn't moved from the front window. His pale eyes studied us as we hurried in.

"Well? What did you find out?" he demanded.

"It's definitely weird over there," Alec told him. We all began talking at once.

"We met a kid named Trevor," I said. "He's pale as a ghost. He looks like a strong wind could blow him away."

"He wouldn't open the door all the way," Alec said. "He didn't want us to see what was going on inside."

"He was just shy," Tricia said. "I think he was tired from unpacking, that's all. He was kind of sweet-looking."

"I could see the three coffins," I said. "They were lined up in the living room. How weird is that?"

Alec added, "And we heard his mother say something about finding food. You know. Like human flesh to eat."

Grandpa Mo shuddered at those words. He hugged himself, his bony arms poking out of his short-sleeved shirt.

"She didn't say that at all," Tricia insisted. "You're making it sound a lot weirder than it really was."

"I knew this would happen," Grandpa Mo uttered, still hugging himself. "I knew it."

"You knew *what* would happen?" a voice demanded. We turned to see Mom walk into the room. She dropped her briefcase on a chair and tossed her jacket on top of it.

She was wearing a pale yellow sweater over a denim skirt. She shook her dark hair back over her shoulder.

"We're talking about the new neighbors," I said. "They're a little weird and —"

"Zombies have moved right next door," Grandpa Mo interrupted. "Right next door to us. And . . . people are going to start dying."

Mom rolled her eyes. "Mo, you have *got* to stop

trying to scare the kids. They're having a hard enough time getting used to their new home. They don't need you telling your crazy zombie stories day and night."

Grandpa Mo turned back to the window. "All my life I've had nightmares about zombies," he said.

"Then why do you want to give the *kids* nightmares?" Mom demanded. She started to pick up her briefcase. "I have a million test papers to grade tonight. I really don't have time —"

"But your new neighbors *are* definitely strange, Mrs. Manzetti," Alec said. "We met this kid. Trevor. And he acted like maybe he was just waking up from being dead a long time. And —"

"Oh, no," Mom groaned. "Alec, does Grandpa Mo have *you* believing in zombies now?"

Alec shrugged. "Well . . ." His face turned red.

"So many nightmares," Grandpa Mo mumbled, gazing out the window. "When I was a child, the dreams were so real, I woke up screaming. I can still picture those zombie dreams."

Mom pointed a finger at him. "Mo, they were just dreams."

Grandpa Mo shook his head. "I'm not so sure. I never wanted to come back to this house. But I had nowhere else to go." He motioned to the window. "I don't feel safe now. I think we should all keep our eyes open."

He made his way out of the room, his arms crossed over his chest.

Mom sighed. "You kids have to understand. He's very old and not well. I'm not saying he's gone a little crazy, but —"

"Mom, there *is* something very strange about the new neighbors," I interrupted. "We watched them move in. They have coffins. Three long wooden coffins."

Mom set her briefcase back down in the chair. She brushed her hair back again. "Coffins? In their house?"

"In their living room," Alec and I said at the same time.

Mom laughed. "You're making that up."

"No way," Alec and I spoke together again.

"I saw them, too," Tricia said. "It's a little strange. But so what?"

"So maybe your grandfather isn't crazy," Alec told her.

Mom crossed to the window and peered out at the house next door. "Hey, look — they're leaving."

We all rushed to the window in time to see a long black car pull down the driveway. The windows were dark. I couldn't see anyone inside.

Mom's green eyes flashed. She grinned. "Do you really think zombies drive a car?" she asked.

"It's possible," Alec said. "Do you believe us about the coffins in the living room?"

"No, I don't," Mom said. "I think that's one of Grandpa Mo's ideas. You probably saw moving cartons."

I grabbed Mom's hand and tugged her to the front door. "The coffins are really coffins," I said. "We didn't make them up. Come on, we'll show you."

Mom pulled back. "You mean, go over there?"

"They just left," I said. "We can peek in the living room window."

"When you see the coffins, will you admit it's totally strange?" Alec asked.

"Yes, I'll admit it," Mom said. "It's totally weird to keep three coffins in your living room. But I don't believe any of you for a minute."

"You'll see," I said. "We're not making it up. And we're not crazy."

I led the way out the front door and across the lawn to their driveway. The afternoon sun was lowering behind the trees of the graveyard. Long shadows stretched in front of us as we walked.

We passed the front stoop. The door was closed. A small cactus plant in a pot stood in a corner of the stoop.

We walked up to the living room window. It was long and low.

I stepped back and let Mom go first. "Go ahead. Look in the living room. You'll see them. You'll see we're not crazy."

Mom pressed her face to the window glass. She shielded her eyes with one hand. She gazed into the house for a long moment.

Then she staggered back with a loud gasp. "I . . . I don't believe it!" she cried. "Yes. I see them. Three coffins. But . . . oh, no. Oh, noooo . . . There's a human skull resting on one of them. And . . . I see . . . I see some kind of creature crawling out of a coffin!"

22

All three of us stared openmouthed at her. Alec was the first to speak. "I *knew* it! Your grandfather was right!"

Mom burst out laughing. She has a booming laugh. When she laughs, her whole body shakes. "Look at you. I can't believe your faces!" she exclaimed. "You actually believed me — didn't you!"

"No way," Tricia said. "I didn't believe it. But Kenny and Alec did."

My heart was still beating a little fast. "Good joke, Mom," I said. "You got me with that one."

"But the coffins . . ." Alec said. "Mrs. Manzetti, what about the coffins?"

Mom swept her hand to the window. "Take a look."

We stepped up to the window and peered into the dimly lit living room. No coffins. The coffins were gone.

"They must have moved them," Alec said.

"Alec, give it a rest," Mom told him. "You had your joke and I had mine." We started back to our house.

My head was spinning. I didn't really know what to think.

I don't believe in zombies or ghosts or anything like that. So why did I get so creeped out about the weird new neighbors and their coffins? It *had* to be because of Grandpa Mo's stories.

We made our way back into the house. "Do you want to stay for dinner?" Mom asked Alec. "Sal is bringing home takeout chicken and French fries."

"Definitely!" Alec exclaimed. Then he added, "I'd better text my mother."

After dinner, we were in the den with the TV on in the background. Alec and I wanted to go back to our *Walking Zombies* game. But Tricia came in with something else on her mind. The Halloween party.

She dropped down on the floor with her back against the couch. "I thought you guys were going to help me get this party together," she said.

"No problem," I said. "What do you want us to do?"

"Everything," she said. "We haven't started. We have no plan. We don't know what we're doing."

"I thought we decided it's going to be a zombie party," Alec said.

"No, we didn't," Tricia replied. "But tell you what . . ."

"What?"

"I'll agree to a zombie party if you two agree to do all the invitations."

Alec and I looked at each other. "Who are we going to invite?" I asked.

"Everyone in our class and the other seventh-grade class," Tricia said. "I mean, that's the whole reason for the party, remember? To make new friends from school?"

"I guess Alec and I can do the inviting," I said.

"If you agree it's an all-zombie party," Alec added.

Before Tricia could answer, something on TV caught my eye. It was a bunch of high school kids. They were standing with a reporter who was holding a microphone up to them. It was a news show.

"Hey, check this out," I said. I turned up the volume. "Why do those teenagers look so frightened?"

We turned to the TV and watched the news report. It didn't take long to find out why those kids were so scared.

23

"Was it a prank? Or was it something a lot more frightening?" the news reporter asked. He was a good-looking young guy with curly blond hair and a nice suntan. He wore a pale blue dress shirt open at the neck and straight-legged jeans.

He continued: "With Halloween approaching, these students from Franklin Village High tell a story that could make for the scariest Halloween ever."

They cut to one of the girls, dark hair tied back in a ponytail, her face excited. "We were passing the graveyard on Ardmore...," she said. "That's where we saw them. We thought they were homeless people camping out in the cemetery."

The news reporter nodded. The girl continued. "But then they started to come after us. And... and we saw their faces. I started to scream."

The reporter turned to the camera. "These shaken teenagers say they were chased by a small horde of staggering, rotting zombies that climbed out of the Ardmore Road Cemetery."

The screen filled with a picture of the cemetery — the one right across from us. The reporter continued:

"Two of these kids are honor students. None of them has ever been in any trouble before."

One of the boys, a big overweight kid with short black hair and a silver ring in one ear, began to speak. "The zombies were grunting and groaning . . . reaching for us. They looked so hungry."

Back to the girl with the ponytail: "Just like zombies on TV. Only they were real. Their skin . . . it was falling off. Some of them had no eyes. It . . . it was like a horror show."

Back to the reporter: "The kids say they ran for their lives. When they were safe, they called 911. Local police are not happy about this. They say they have enough *real* problems on their hands without having to deal with Halloween pranks.

"But the kids will not be charged. These five teens are convinced it was *not* a prank. They all believe this is the beginning of the zombie apocalypse we hear so much about. But I'm not so sure I believe their story — not this close to Halloween."

The girl with the ponytail frowned at him. "I know what I saw," she said. "They are here!"

The three of us stared in silence at the TV for a long while. The news show continued, but I didn't hear a word they were saying.

Finally, I clicked it off and turned to Tricia and Alec. "That is totally awesome!" I said.

Alec's mouth dropped open. "Huh? Why?"

"Those high school kids," I said. "They got themselves on TV."

Tricia was squeezing a couch pillow between her hands. She squinted at me. "You think it was a joke?"

"Definitely," I said. "Of *course* it was a joke."

"No way," Alec said. "Did you see how scared they looked?"

"They're probably all in drama class," I said. "They were totally acting. It was a class project."

Alec jumped up and began pacing back and forth. He looked tense, his hands balled into tight fists. "It wasn't a joke, Kenny," he said.

"One of the kids would have smiled or winked or something. But you saw their faces. They were terrified."

"But, Alec —"

"And it happened right across the street. It was just like what your grandfather has been telling us. And it happened right across the street."

"Whoa. Easy, Alec," Tricia said. "You're going to bust a blood vessel."

I laughed. "And then *Alec* would become a zombie."

He let out a hoarse cry. "I . . . I don't understand why you two are just sitting there acting calm like nothing happened. I believe what they said. Those teenagers saw *real* zombies right across the street."

I shook my head. I started to answer. But an idea flashed into my mind.

It was probably a bad idea. Tricia would think it was totally stupid. But I knew Alec would like it.

"Do you want to be on TV?" I asked.

Alec stopped pacing. "Maybe . . ."

"I've got an awesome idea," I said. "How about we get a bunch of kids together, and we start a zombie patrol."

Tricia burst out laughing. "You could wear big Zs on your shirts. And maybe wear a cape and red tights."

"Ha-ha. You're so funny," I said sarcastically.

"What would the zombie patrol do?" Alec asked. His voice cracked. I could see he was scared.

"Well, we'd patrol Franklin Village," I said. "And search for the zombies that scared those high school kids."

Alec shook his head. "I don't know, Kenny. If the zombies really are here..." His voice trailed off.

Tricia jumped up from the couch and went racing upstairs.

"Where are you going?" I shouted.

"You'll see. Be right back."

A few seconds later, she returned to the den carrying the butterfly net she'd used for a science project. "Here, Kenny." She handed it to me.

"What's this for?" I asked.

She grinned. "It's a zombie catcher. You just swing the net over the zombie's head." She laughed again.

I tossed it to the floor. "Did anyone ever tell you how funny you are?" I snapped.

"Yes," she said.

"They were wrong," I said. I turned back to Alec. "So? What do you think of my idea? After that news story, our patrol is sure to get us on TV. And in the newspaper, and everywhere. It'll go viral. You'll see."

"You just think it's a big joke," Alec said. "But I don't."

"But we could have fun," I protested. "We'll say we want to protect our town. Everyone will know us. We'll be famous!"

Tricia picked up the butterfly net. "Kenny, why do you want to do this crazy thing?" she demanded. "It's not like you at all."

"Give me a break. It's Halloween," I said. "Why not have some fun?"

"Well . . . maybe," Alec said finally.

And that's how the zombie patrol got started. It was fun for one week — until we found our first *real zombies*.

Then, we knew we were in terrible danger.

PART THREE

FIVE DAYS TILL HALLOWEEN

25

"I'm not really hungry tonight," Grandpa Mo said.

"Don't you like your hamburger?" Mom asked, studying him from across the dinner table. "Should I make you something else?"

"Aren't you feeling well, Pops?" my dad asked, still chewing his burger.

Grandpa Mo had a faraway look in his eyes. I'd noticed it as soon as we sat down to dinner. His white hair, usually perfectly brushed back, stood up in clumps. His face seemed even paler than usual, pale and powdery.

"I've been having the zombie dreams again," he said, shaking his head. "They keep me up at night."

Dad dabbed a paper napkin at his mouth. "You have to keep reminding yourself they are just dreams, Pops," he said.

"They seem more than dreams, Sal," Grandpa Mo told him. "They seem like real life."

"I remember how vivid your dreams were, even when I was a kid," Dad said.

Grandpa Mo kept his eyes on the window. It looked out to the graveyard across the street. "The zombies . . . They want me," he said softly, as if he was talking to himself. "They are desperate to get me. Sometimes in my dream . . . Sometimes I can feel their hands wrap around my wrists and try to pull me from my bed."

"Uh . . . Pops?" Dad tried to get his attention. But Grandpa Mo's mind had drifted far away.

"Their hands are so hard," he said. "Hard and brittle and cold . . . They grab me. They try to pull me with them."

"Just dreams," Mom said.

Dad climbed to his feet and walked around the table to Grandpa Mo. "Here. Let me help you up," he said. "Why don't you take a rest? I'll wake you up for some ice cream later."

Grandpa Mo nodded. He let Dad guide him out of the dining room.

Shaking her head, Mom went into the kitchen for some more salad.

Tricia and Alec sat across from me. Alec was staying for dinner for the third night in a row. He said his parents were vegetarians, and he never got anything good to eat at home.

"Grandpa Mo is having one of his bad days," Tricia said.

Alec swallowed a chunk of hamburger. "Kenny, do you think we should tell him about our zombie patrol? Might cheer him up or something."

"Sshhh." I put a finger to my mouth. "No way," I whispered. "And I'm not telling Mom and Dad, either. You know what they'll say. They'll say it's too dangerous."

"And stupid," Tricia chimed in.

I threw an onion ring at her. Missed, and it dropped to the floor.

"Dad already keeps telling me to spend less time on zombie nonsense and more time on my homework," I whispered to Alec. "We have to keep the patrol a secret."

"*What's* a secret?" Mom asked, walking back into the room with the salad bowl in her hands.

"I can't tell you," I said. "It's a secret."

She laughed. "You don't have secrets from your parents — *do* you, Kenny?"

"Of course not," I said.

After dinner, Tricia, Alec, and I went down to the basement. We moved some of the cartons and old furniture to the wall and started to plan the decorations for our Halloween party.

Tricia was excited. She liked parties. But Alec and I had other things on our minds.

Late that night, I couldn't fall asleep. I kept thinking about the zombie patrol.

So far, Alec and I had four other guys who wanted to be in the group. We planned to meet for our first patrol tomorrow night after dinner.

The others all believed that there might be real zombies in Franklin Village. I was the only one who didn't think so.

I promised them we'd get on the TV news. Now as I lay there, gazing up at the shadows on my ceiling, I kept thinking: *What if they're right and I'm wrong? Is this zombie patrol idea of mine totally dangerous?*

I was finally starting to feel sleepy at two in the morning when I heard a low moan outside my bedroom window.

At first, I thought it was a dog. But the second moan sounded like a human cry.

I sat straight up, wide awake now. And listened. It was a warm night for October, and my bedroom window was open.

Was the cry coming from the graveyard?

A chill rolled down my back.

Another cry. This one sounded like, *"Help meeeee."*

I jumped from my bed. My feet tangled in the covers, and I fell to the floor. The sound of the cry from outside stayed in my ears.

I pulled myself up and stumbled to the window.

"Help meeee."

I pushed the curtains aside and poked my head out of the window. The air felt warm and damp.

A bright half-moon sent silvery light washing over the graveyard across the street. The tombstones appeared to gleam in the light.

I blinked a few times, waiting for my eyes to adjust to the gray light. Squinting across the street, I saw someone. Someone in the graveyard.

I struggled to focus my eyes. A string of clouds stretched over the moon, casting the graveyard in deep shadow.

Then the clouds rolled past, and the ground brightened again.

And I saw the figure dressed in white, some kind of flowing white gown.

What was he doing among the tombstones? Was he dancing?

His arms rose up and down. He appeared to float in the white gown. Float along the crooked row of graves.

"Help meeeee."

As he uttered the shrill cry, he continued his eerie dance.

I realized I'd stopped breathing. My eyes on the ghostly figure, I forced myself to take a deep breath.

My hands gripped the windowsill tightly, as if I'd fall through the floor if I let go.

I struggled to calm my mind, to stop the frightening thoughts that whirred past.

A ghost. A ghost or a zombie dancing in the graveyard.

Was it one of the zombies that chased those kids? A zombie all in white?

And then the moonlight grew even brighter. And everything became clearer, like a camera finding its focus.

And I saw the face of the dancing ghost. Saw it clearly. The pale eyes. The white hair.

Grandpa Mo.

26

I stopped breathing again. I gripped the windowsill so tightly, my hands ached. I lurched backward, away from the window . . . away from the frightening sight of my grandfather floating along the tombstones.

Then I spun around and ran down the hall to my parents' room. "Mom! Dad!" I screamed. I pounded their door with my fist.

After a few seconds, the door swung open. Dad poked his head out, blinking, his hair down over his eyes. "Kenny? Are you okay?"

"It . . . It's Grandpa Mo!" I choked out. "Hurry. You've got to come. He . . . he's in the graveyard."

Dad blinked some more. "What time is it?"

"It doesn't matter, Dad," I said. I tugged at his pajama sleeve. "Grandpa Mo is in the graveyard. We have to get him."

Dad shook his head hard, as if clearing his mind. "My slippers," he said. He disappeared for a few seconds. Then he hurtled out into the hall, in his striped pajamas, bedroom slippers on his feet.

The two of us ran out of the house. I knew Grandpa Mo was in trouble. Something strange was happening to him. His wailing cries for help repeated in my brain.

Dad and I ran across the street. His slippers made a *clack-clack* sound on the pavement as he ran. I realized I was barefoot. The street felt cold under my feet. But I didn't care. I just wanted to reach Grandpa Mo — before something terrible happened to him.

Dad and I ran under the trees at the edge of the graveyard. Above us, the leaves whispered and rattled.

The moonlight sent darting shadows all around us. The ground was hard dirt and weeds. Something scratched the bottom of my left foot, but I didn't stop.

Grandpa Mo was at the far end of the row of tombstones. His white robe glowed in the moonlight. He was twisting around, his eyes rolling in his head.

I ran up to him, crying his name. "Grandpa Mo! Grandpa Mo!"

He turned his face toward me, but he didn't seem to recognize me. His eyes were so pale, they appeared solid white. His chin trembled.

His hair fluttered above his head in the steady breeze.

Dad came running up to us, gasping for breath. He took Grandpa Mo by the shoulder. Grandpa Mo stared blankly at him.

"Pops, you shouldn't be out here," Dad said. "Come with us. Kenny and I will take you home."

Grandpa Mo nodded. But I still wasn't sure he knew who we were.

He was wearing his white bathrobe. Dad saw that it was coming open, so he tightened the belt for Grandpa Mo. Without another word, we led him back to the house.

Mom and Tricia were waiting in the kitchen. We sat Grandpa Mo down at the kitchen table. "Mo, I'll make you a cup of that green tea you like," Mom said.

My grandfather nodded. He had one arm on the table. He rested his head in his hand. "I had a dream," he said.

Dad sat down next to him. "A dream?"

Grandpa Mo nodded again. "I dreamed the zombies came for me again. They pulled me out of bed. They forced me out into the dark night. They . . . they . . ."

"Take it easy, Pops," Dad said, patting Grandpa Mo's shoulder.

"I dreamed I was in the graveyard," the old man said. "I dreamed I was dancing along the graves. They forced me, Sal. They forced me to dance along the graves."

Grandpa Mo rubbed his chin. It made a dry, scratchy sound. He raised his eyes to my dad. "Isn't that a strange dream? Dreaming I was in the graveyard?"

Dad glanced at Mom. Like he didn't know what to say. He turned to Grandpa Mo. "It wasn't a dream, Pops," he said. "Kenny and I . . . We found you there. Remember?"

"It *was* a dream," Grandpa Mo insisted. "I dreamed I was in the graveyard."

Tricia pulled me into the hall and whispered, "Well, that's something new. Grandpa Mo must be a sleepwalker."

"A sleepwalker?"

"He was sound asleep and dreaming," Tricia whispered. "He walked to the graveyard in his sleep."

I squinted at Grandpa Mo at the kitchen table. He had the teacup between his hands, but he wasn't drinking the tea. He was still blinking and shaking his head.

I thought about what Tricia had said. But then another idea flashed into my mind.

"What if he wasn't dreaming?" I whispered to Tricia. "What if it was real? You know, some zombies have mind control. It's in the TV show and the game. What if zombies used their mind control to force him to the graveyard? What if he's telling the truth?"

Tricia raised a fist — and clonked the top of my head with it.

"Hey — why'd you do that?" I cried.

"To knock some sense in your head, Kenny. Don't start believing this stuff."

I gazed at Grandpa Mo, so pale, his white hair wild above his face, the teacup trembling in his hand. His eyes had a faraway look. They seemed to be seeing things we couldn't see.

I gazed at Grandpa Mo — and I didn't know what to believe.

Something is wrong here, I told myself. *There's something I don't understand.*

What if he is under some kind of spell? What if the zombies control him now?

Was I being crazy?

Was I letting my imagination run away with me?

I hoped so. But . . . for the first time in my life, I felt a little afraid of Grandpa Mo.

27

The next night after dinner, the zombie patrol met for our first adventure. We met in front of Alec's house because I was afraid my parents might find out about it.

There were six of us, including Alec and me. The other four were all guys from our class. Munroe Ferber, Travis Costanza, Sammy White, and Jeremy Bodner.

Jeremy kept us waiting about twenty minutes. He said he had to sneak out through his bedroom window because his parents would never allow him to go out like this at night.

Munroe told his dad he had to do a class project: gazing at the stars. Munroe is a short, stumpy kid with big, round eyes and a funny, deep croaky voice. He says he hates it when kids call him by his nickname — Frog.

Travis and Sammy are best friends who live somewhere on the other side of the graveyard. These guys all joined the patrol, I guess, because they're huge fans of *The Walking Zombies*. And because Alec and I promised we'd get on TV.

We hung out behind Alec's garage, not talking much. I think everyone was a little tense.

When Jeremy finally arrived, everyone started to talk at once.

"Are we really doing this? You really think we'll see zombies?"

"Aren't we just doing this to get on TV? Alec told us we'll be on the news."

"Why don't we just go to my house and play *The Walking Zombies*? I have the new beta version three that hasn't been released."

"Awesome. How did you get it?"

"I'm not allowed to tell."

"What do we do if we see some zombies?"

"Scream."

"Run?"

"Hit them in the head with a shovel."

"We don't have a shovel."

"Guys, let's get it together," I said. "It's getting late. Let's start our patrol at the graveyard."

"Why? Do we really have to go in there?" Sammy asked. He was a big dude. He was at least a head taller than me. But he had a whiny voice, and he seemed to be the biggest chicken.

"It just seems like if you want to see zombies, you should start at a graveyard," I said.

The others agreed. We started to walk along Ardmore Road toward the cemetery entrance.

It had rained for most of the afternoon. The ground was muddy and soft. The lawns glistened under the light of the low half-moon. We stepped around puddles on the street.

Sammy strode up beside Alec and me. "Are you sure this is going to get us on TV?" he demanded.

Before I could answer, Travis chimed in. "I think we need uniforms. I mean, like totally awesome zombie patrol uniforms."

"Sweet," Jeremy said. "I saw these Navy SEAL uniforms. With these awesome boots. Maybe we could get someone to copy them and —"

"We can't afford uniforms and boots," I said. "You don't need uniforms to hunt for zombies."

Alec nodded his head in agreement.

"What if we just have some cool T-shirts made?" Jeremy said. "There's that place at the mall that does T-shirts really cheap."

"They could be black with ZP on the front in red," Sammy said.

"No. They have to be FVZP," Travis told him.

I stared at him. "FVZP? What does that stand for?"

"Franklin Village Zombie Patrol."

A dark SUV rumbled past. A kid stared out the back window at us. He stuck his tongue out as he passed. The tires splashed rainwater over the curb.

The half-moon disappeared behind a heavy curtain of clouds. Everything grew darker, like the lights going down in a movie theater. We had reached the entrance gate to the cemetery.

"We should definitely have membership cards," Travis said. "And maybe a secret handshake? It could be something like this." He grabbed Jeremy's hand and pumped it up and down.

"Whoa! Stop right there!" I cried. I trotted to the front of the group. I turned to face them and raised both hands to signal *halt*. "You guys have a bad attitude," I said. "Do you want to find some zombies or not?"

"No. We want to get on TV," Munroe answered.

The other guys laughed.

"Well, we're not going to get on TV because of our uniforms or our T-shirts, or our membership cards," I said. "We need a story to tell. We need to find some zombies. Something to tell the news reporter."

"I stepped in a puddle," Jeremy said. "Look. My jeans are soaked."

"It's going to be muddy in the graveyard," Sammy said. "Maybe we should patrol somewhere else."

"It got too dark," Munroe muttered. "What happened to the moon?"

"I brought a flashlight," I said. I pulled it from my backpack. "Come on, dudes. No more talk.

We *have* to start the patrol in the graveyard. The TV news guys will love it."

"Follow Kenny and me," Alec said, "and stick close together."

They grumbled a little more. But Alec and I ignored them. We tugged open the iron gate and made our way into the graveyard.

I gazed up at the sky. The clouds were heavy and black. The moon was lost behind them. I clicked on the flashlight. It was a halogen flashlight and it shone a bright white circle over the rows of graves.

Alec and I started to follow the light down the first row of graves. I aimed the white beam from stone to stone. These graves were old, and the stones tilted back as if blown by the wind.

My shoes sank into the soft mud as I walked. I tried to ignore the cold water that seeped into my socks.

It was silent here. The only sounds were the soft *plop* of our footsteps in the mud. The only thing moving were the tall, old trees. Their branches quaked and groaned overhead.

I gazed up. I wished the moonlight would return. But the sky seemed to grow even blacker.

Alec stumbled over a raised tree root. I grabbed him before he fell. He steadied himself quickly. His eyes followed my beam of light.

"I don't see anything." His voice came out in a whisper. "Nothing moving here."

We turned at the end of the row and followed a low hill to the next group of graves. My light swept up and down the crooked tombstones.

"The dead are sleeping soundly tonight," Alec whispered.

I turned the light on him. It was a cold October night. But he had drops of sweat across his forehead.

I suddenly pictured Grandpa Mo in this graveyard late last night. The sleeves of his white robe flying up as he danced between the tombstones.

No. I'm not like Alec. I don't believe in zombies. No way. I just want to have a little excitement.

Alec and I climbed the hill, slipping on the wet grass on the path. A gust of wind made the trees shake and rattle all around us.

I suddenly remembered the other four guys. I didn't hear them. They must have fallen behind.

I spun around. "Hey, dudes? Let's stick together, okay?"

I couldn't see them.

"Hey, dudes? Munroe? Jeremy?" My voice came out muffled against the wind. I cupped my hands around my mouth and shouted again.

No reply. No sign of them.

I shone my light down the hill. I swept it back and forth.

"Where are they?" Alec asked, his voice shrill with worry. "They couldn't just disappear."

"Come on," I said. I motioned him down the hill. We retraced our steps. I kept the light darting from side to side.

"Hey, guys!" I shouted as loudly as I could. "Where are you? Come on. This isn't funny. Where are you?"

No answer.

A chill tightened the back of my neck. My mouth suddenly felt dry.

I turned to Alec. Even in the darkness, I could see the fear on his face.

"S-something happened to them," I said.

He nodded. But he didn't say a word. He stood beside me, breathing hard.

And then we heard loud, frantic scraping. We both turned — and gasped when we saw something climb from behind a tall gravestone.

28

Alec saw it, too. He squeezed the arm of my jacket. We both stumbled back and tried to hide behind a fat tree trunk.

The tree smelled damp and moldy. I didn't care. I grabbed on to it. Hid behind it. And watched the creature slither out from the grave and make its way onto the grassy path.

What was it? It was moving so slowly, as if waking up from being dead. It turned and began to lope down the hill.

My heart pounded. I had to force myself to breathe.

"What *is* that?" I whispered.

"The light," Alec whispered back, lifting my arm.

I'd forgotten I was holding it. I raised the flashlight and aimed the beam at the creature's back.

As soon as the light swept over it, it spun around.

I stared at its face. And gasped.

"Trevor!" I choked out. "Hey — Trevor! What are you doing here?"

"I don't believe it," Alec whispered. "Your weird next-door neighbor."

He waved his hands in front of his face, shielding his eyes.

I lowered the beam of light. Alec and I walked over to him. "Trevor? Hi. Remember us? Kenny and Alec? I live next door?"

He nodded. "Hey," he said softly. He pulled up the black hood of his hoodie.

"What are you doing here?" Alec repeated the question.

"What are *you* doing out here?" Trevor shot back. He didn't smile. His eyes studied us coldly.

"We . . . started a patrol," I said. "To . . . uh . . . hunt for zombies."

He thought about it for a moment. "It's like a game?"

"No," Alec said. "For real. Did you see the news story about those high school kids? They say they were chased by zombies from this cemetery."

Trevor shook his head. "But . . . it's a game, right? I mean, do you really believe in zombies?"

"Well . . . yes," Alec said.

I checked out Trevor's hoodie and jeans. They weren't covered in mud. He hadn't climbed out of a grave. He was just walking behind the gravestones.

But why?

"Did you see four other guys out here?" Alec asked. "They're in our patrol."

Trevor shook his head again. His face seemed to disappear inside the hoodie. "No. I didn't see anyone."

He squinted at us. "You really believe there might be zombies in Franklin Village?"

"Maybe," I said. "We just thought we'd patrol at night and search for them."

"But that could be dangerous," Trevor said. He leaned toward us. His eyes darted from Alec to me. "That could be *very* dangerous."

A chill rolled down my back. He had suddenly changed. His voice deepened. And his words sounded like a warning.

Or a *threat*.

I took a step back. Under the black hoodie, he had a menacing look on his face.

"We'll be careful," I said.

"You should be very careful," Trevor said.

Another threat?

"Do you want to join us?" Alec blurted out. "Join our zombie patrol?"

"I don't think so," he answered quickly. "I don't think it's a good idea."

"We're just going out on patrol a few nights," I said. "Maybe you could come along. . . ."

"No, I can't. And I think you should stop . . . before you get in trouble." He turned and started down the hill, taking long strides, hands in his jeans pockets.

"Hey, wait!" I shouted. "What were *you* doing here?"

"Taking a walk," he called back. Then he vanished into the darkness.

Alec and I stood in silence for a long moment. I kept repeating in my mind what Trevor had said. And I kept seeing those dark eyes, that threatening expression.

"Weird dude," Alec said. "He gives me the creeps. Seriously."

"I thought I saw him climb out of a grave," I said.

"But he wasn't muddy or anything," Alec replied.

"But why wouldn't he tell us what he was doing out here?" I said. "I don't believe he was just taking a walk."

"I keep thinking about the three coffins in his house," Alec said. "One for each member of the family."

"Wish we could check those coffins out," I said.

Alec gazed around. "Where is everyone else? What happened to the other guys? I'm worried about them. Seriously."

"This is too scary. Let's go home," I said.

We started down the path. Blown by the swirling wind, the grass swayed one way, then the other. The trees shivered and creaked. I felt as if the whole graveyard had suddenly come to life.

And then I saw another figure come crashing out from behind a gravestone. Something big and dark. Roaring toward us on all fours.

Its red eyes glowed in the blackness. And a menacing growl exploded from its throat.

I froze in terror. The flashlight fell from my hand.

I glimpsed it clearly just before it attacked. Just before it leaped on me, eyes glowing, gnashing its teeth.

Just before it knocked me onto my back and lowered its head to devour me.

29

"Down!" Alec screamed. "Down, boy!"

Alec dove forward and tried to pull the huge, snarling dog off me.

The big creature had me pinned to the ground. It slobbered hot drool down on my face as it snapped its teeth at me.

"Down! Get off!" Alec screamed over the growls and panting breaths of the enormous black dog. He grabbed it around the middle and tugged it off me.

With a furious snarl, the dog turned on Alec.

Alec tried to back away — but he stumbled over a low gravestone.

He scrambled to his feet as the dog arched its back, preparing to leap.

Still shaking, wiping the thick, warm dog drool off my cheeks, I had a desperate idea. I reached into my jeans pockets with a trembling hand.

I wrapped my fingers around the pack and pulled out my Zombie Goop Loops. "Here!" I cried at the top of my lungs. "Here! Hungry?"

I held out the package. Waved it in front of the growling dog's snout.

Then I tossed it to the ground in front of the creature. The Goop Loops spilled out onto the grass.

Would the dog go for them? Would it decide to eat them instead of Alec and me?

I didn't wait to find out. "Let's go!" I cried.

I pulled Alec to his feet, and we both took off running down the sloping grass toward the front gate.

I glanced back as I ran. Yes. The dog had its face lowered to the ground. It was chomping away, slurping up the zombie candy loops.

A brilliant victory for Kenny Manzetti!

Alec and I ran faster than we'd ever run. Our shoes pounded the wet ground like drumbeats. We raced through the cemetery gate and across the street. We almost ran right into two teenage girls riding slowly side-by-side down the sidewalk on bikes.

"Hey — what's your problem?" one of them shouted at us.

"Zombies!" Alec shouted back.

I don't know why he said that. I guess it was the first thing that popped into his mind.

We darted into my house and carefully closed the front door behind us. We were halfway up the stairs to my room when Dad stepped into the hallway behind us.

"Hey, guys," he called. "What's up?"

I was still struggling to slow my heartbeat, still trying to catch my breath. "Uh . . . Alec came over to help me with my science notebook," I said, hoping I sounded normal.

"No zombie video games tonight?" Dad asked.

"No. It's a school night," Alec answered.

I felt bad lying to Dad. But I didn't want my parents to know about the zombie patrol. Alec and I piled into my room and shut the door behind us.

We had survived the dog attack, thanks to Zombie Goop Loops. But Alec had a long scratch on one arm, and the pocket was ripped on his new down jacket.

Alec tossed his jacket onto the floor in front of my bed. "It's just a scratch," he said. "What about our four friends? Shouldn't we call 911 and report them missing?"

"Maybe we should call their parents," I said. "Or . . . maybe we should tell *my* parents. This is too serious to keep quiet about. I mean, those four guys just vanished. One minute they were behind us in the graveyard. The next minute . . ."

My voice trailed off. I felt sick thinking about it. Four guys disappeared into thin air. And it was all our fault. I thought I might toss my dinner.

"Maybe you *should* tell your parents," Alec said softly. He shook his head. "I . . . hope the guys are okay. I just have this bad feeling . . ."

The doorbell sound chimed on my phone. A text message.

I pulled the phone from my jeans. I raised the screen to my eyes.

I read it quickly.

"Oh, nooo!" I cried. "I don't *believe* it!"

Gripping my phone tightly, I read the text message again. Then I turned to Alec. "It's from Munroe," I said.

"Read it to me," Alec replied.

"That was 2 scary. We all went home. How about we start a Star Wars *club instead?"*

Alec blinked. Then he burst out laughing. "Do you believe those big chickens?"

"At least they're okay," I said. "But I can't believe they just ran away. I thought they wanted to be on TV."

"You and I will be the zombie patrol," Alec said. "We don't need them." He picked up his jacket and started to pull it on. "When do you want to go out again? Tomorrow night?"

"I don't think so," I said. "Mom and Dad —"

"Maybe this weekend," Alec said. "Maybe we'll have better luck."

Alec left, and I got changed for bed. But I couldn't get to sleep. I was still wired from my mad run to escape the angry dog. I couldn't get my heartbeats to slow down to normal. My body felt cold and tingly all over.

I shut my eyes, and everything that happened tonight kept rolling past me, repeating and repeating like a video on a loop. I kept seeing the graves under the moonlight, poking up from the muddy ground.

And I saw Trevor stepping out from behind a gravestone. . . . Trevor, so strange and unfriendly. What was he doing there, walking by himself in the cemetery at night?

I knew what Alec and I were doing. We had a reason to be there. But why was Trevor there? We asked him, but he wouldn't tell us.

And did he threaten us? Did he threaten us when he said how dangerous hunting zombies could be? Was that some kind of hint?

The red-eyed dog ran past my shut eyes. Again, I heard its furious snarls and felt the hot slobber from its gnashing mouth splash my face.

I was still wide awake when I heard the ugly moans from outside my open bedroom window. I sat straight up and listened. The curtains were blowing softly in a steady breeze.

And over the sound of the wind I heard another long, low moan. Like a person in pain. I climbed out of bed and crossed to the window.

Another moan, followed by shrill cries.

I pushed the curtains away and peered out.

The frightening sounds were definitely coming from Trevor's house next door. I stuck my head farther out the window. The lights in his house were all off.

But again, I heard an eerie moan: "Owoooooooooooh."

I swallowed hard. The cold night air made me tremble.

I have to see what's happening over there, I decided.

I picked up the jeans I'd tossed on the floor and pulled them over my pajama pants. Then I found a pair of flip-flops by my closet.

I made my way down the hall without making a sound. Grandpa Mo had his door closed. But I was surprised to see that his light was still on. I guessed he couldn't sleep, either.

I went down the stairs on tiptoe so the steps wouldn't creak and wake Tricia or my parents. I pulled open the front door and stepped outside. The half-moon was smaller now and high in the sky. The wind was swirling the dead leaves in the front yard.

Hugging myself against the cold, I crossed the front yard and crept up to Trevor's house. I stopped when I heard another eerie cry, louder now. Coming from inside the house.

My legs didn't want to move. My heart thudded in my chest.

I forced myself to sneak up to the front window. I bent low so I wouldn't be seen. Pale gray light poured out from the living room.

I took a deep breath, raised myself — and peered into the house.

30

It took my eyes a few seconds to adjust to the dim light inside the room. When I could finally focus, I saw Trevor sprawled on a couch. His head was propped up on two pillows.

The gray light was pouring from the TV. Trevor was wide awake, staring at the screen.

I turned and saw what he was watching. *The Walking Zombies.*

A long, low moan came from the TV as the zombies swarmed around a group of helpless victims. I'd already seen this episode. It was a good one. Trevor seemed to enjoy it, too. I saw him laugh out loud when the zombies attacked and began to feed on the people.

He shifted on the couch, and I ducked below the window ledge. I waited a few seconds to make sure he hadn't spotted me. Then, staying bent over, I ran back to my house with the moans and cries from the TV show following me.

Back in my room, I couldn't stop shivering. I

dove under the covers to try to warm up. I lay there staring at the ceiling, trying to calm down.

Now I was totally confused about Trevor. It was totally normal to watch *The Walking Zombies*. That didn't prove anything about him.

But he laughed so hard when the living people were being eaten. What did that mean? That he had a twisted sense of humor? Or just that he liked to watch zombies?

So did Alec and I.

I didn't know what to think. I knew I'd be awake all night.

A short while later, I heard a door slam. I heard low voices outside.

Again, I jumped up and rushed to my bedroom window. Trevor's porch light had been turned on. In its glow, I saw Trevor and his parents walking down their driveway.

Where were they going this time of night?

The three of them walked quickly. I couldn't see their faces. Trevor's parents were tall and thin. Their heads were covered by their coat hoods.

They turned left on the street and disappeared down the block.

"Weird," I muttered. "All three of them going out for a midnight walk?"

Then I realized this was my chance. My chance to sneak into their house and uncover the mystery of the three coffins.

What was I looking for? I wasn't sure. But I hoped I'd find some kind of clue.

I thought of calling Alec. But I knew he'd be sound asleep. No way his parents would let him leave the house.

I pulled on the jeans and the flip-flops again. *Should I wake Tricia?*

No. She'd only tell me I'm an idiot and I should go back to sleep.

Okay. Okay. Trevor and his parents were gone. It would be easy — and quick — to see what was in those coffins.

I *had* to know. I *had* to know if three zombies were living right next door to me.

Poor Grandpa Mo was so frightened. It would be good for him to know the truth, too.

Once again, I crept outside.

The swirling winds had stopped. All was still. And silent.

This time, I crept across the driveway and ran over the wet grass, my flip-flops slipping and sliding. I made it to the back of their house.

I could see a dim light in the kitchen window. A screened-in porch ran along the back of the house. I tried the porch door, and it opened easily.

I'm not really breaking in, I told myself. *I'm just going to take a look around and run right out. I won't touch a thing — except for the coffins.*

The kitchen door wasn't locked. I pushed it open silently and crept inside.

31

The kitchen smelled nice. Some kind of spices were in the air. I glanced around quickly. It looked like a normal kitchen.

I could feel the blood pulsing at my temples. *Am I really doing this? Am I really poking around in my neighbors' house after midnight?*

I had to know the truth about this family. I darted into the hall and peeked into the living room.

The TV was still on. I recognized an *Indiana Jones* movie with Harrison Ford. I glanced at the couch where Trevor had been watching the zombie show. The furniture was all big and heavy. Dark wood and big pillows everywhere. Very old-fashioned looking.

No sign of the coffins.

I turned and walked down the long back hall. It's a good thing the hall lights were on. I would have tripped over the big paintings on the floor, tilted against the wall.

The family had just moved in. I guessed they hadn't time to hang the paintings yet. I glanced at them as I passed. They were all portraits of stern-looking old people, all dressed in black. No one smiled.

The bedroom doors were open. I stuck my head in each one. The rooms were all filled with heavy, dark, old-fashioned furniture. One bedroom had stacks of unopened moving cartons up to the ceiling.

I stopped at Trevor's room. I saw a bed with a dark bedspread, a dresser, and a small desk. No posters or anything on the walls. A low bookshelf under the window was completely empty.

I guessed Trevor hadn't had time to unpack his stuff, either.

Still no coffins.

Where were they? *Where?*

This was taking longer than I planned. I realized I was breathing loudly. My legs felt rubbery. I had to force them to keep moving.

The house was all one floor. No upstairs. But was there a basement?

Yes. The basement door was open at the end of the long hall. I peered down the steps. Pitch-black down there — and I didn't think to bring a flashlight.

Should I risk it? Should I turn on the basement light?

It was the only part of the house I hadn't seen.

The only place where the three coffins could be hidden.

My hand fumbled at the switch on the wall. It took three tries, but I clicked the light on.

The stairs were steep and creaked as I made my way down. The air grew cooler and damp. The only sounds were my wheezing breaths.

At the bottom of the steps, I glanced around. The basement was long and narrow. I saw that it was completely carpeted in a dark red carpet.

Moving cartons were stacked along the back wall. I saw several big chairs, a couch, a pile of large, colorful pillows. And in the center of the long room . . .

In the center of the room, lined up side by side . . . I saw the three coffins. The dark wood gleamed under the ceiling lights. The coffins were shut. Their curved lids were smooth and shiny.

I'd found them. I couldn't breathe. I had to *force* the air in and out.

Did I really have the courage to open one?

Don't think about it, Kenny. Just do *it.*

One voice in my head told me to grab a coffin lid and push it open.

Another voice in my head said I should *run.*

But it was too late to run. I was here, and the coffins sat right in front of me.

I stepped up to the closest coffin. It had a sweet wood smell, like it had just been polished.

I walked around to the front. I lowered my hands to the lid.

I tightened them and started to push the lid open. But I stopped when I heard a scraping sound. Then a cough.

I turned to the stairs — and saw Trevor staring at me from the bottom step.

"What are *you* doing here?" he demanded.

32

My heart skipped a beat. I felt my knees start to buckle. A wave of dizziness swept over me. I thought I was about to faint.

I tried to speak, but no sound came out.

What could I say? I was caught. *Caught by a zombie? Trapped in a zombie's basement?*

"Kenny, what are you doing here?" Trevor repeated, taking a few steps toward me. His eyes appeared to glow under the ceiling lights. His face was still buried in his hoodie. But I could see the grim, threatening expression on his face.

"Well ... I ... I ..."

I stammered and stuttered. I couldn't think of an excuse.

Had he returned to climb into his coffin? Returned and found me here?

Was he angry that I knew his secret?

What would he do to me?

I gazed around, searching for an escape route. But he was blocking the way to the stairs.

His glowing eyes locked on mine. I felt he was trying to see into my brain.

He tossed the hood back as he stared at me. Then he said, "Oh. I get it. I get it now."

"Trevor, I . . . I'm sorry," I choked out, my whole body shaking.

"I get it," he repeated. "You want to know what's in the coffins."

"Well . . ." I still couldn't talk. This was the most terrifying, embarrassing moment of my life.

"That's it, right?" Trevor demanded. "It's the coffins. You saw the movers bring them in, and you want to know what's in them?"

I managed to nod.

"Well, go ahead," Trevor said, motioning to the first coffin. "Go ahead, Kenny. Open them up. Take a look."

I stared at him openmouthed. "Uh . . . Really?"

He motioned again.

I took a deep breath. Lowered my hands to the coffin lid. And shoved it open.

33

I pushed the heavy coffin lid all the way up and stared down at its contents. I saw piles of shirts and sweaters, neatly folded and stacked.

Huh?

"Go ahead," Trevor said. "Open the next one, Kenny." He had stepped up beside me. He helped me lower the coffin lid. Then he led the way around to the front of the second coffin.

"Well? Go ahead," he urged. "It's why you came down here — right?"

I pushed open the lid. I saw stacks of old books in this coffin. The coffin was filled to the top with books.

I took a step back. "Trevor, I . . . I'm sorry," I stammered. "I . . . don't know what to say. I —"

"You want me to explain what the coffins are doing down here?" Trevor demanded. "My family owned a funeral parlor. In Birmingham. You know, the next town over. But they lost their lease."

I shook my head. "I'm really sorry. I didn't know —"

"My parents had to close their business," Trevor continued. "They were stuck with these expensive coffins. They tried to find someone to buy them. But no one was interested."

He closed the second coffin lid. "So . . . my parents decided to use them for storage." He gave me a strange, lopsided smile. "That's the whole story, Kenny."

I didn't know what to say. I stood there staring at him. Talk about *awkward*. I really wanted to fall through the floor and disappear. "S-sorry," I choked out again.

He narrowed his eyes at me. "What did *you* think was in the coffins?" he demanded.

I shrugged. No way I could tell him the truth. That I was trying to find some clues that his family were zombies.

"Dead bodies?" he said. "Did you think we had dead bodies in the coffins?"

"No," I said. "I was just curious, that's all. I saw the coffins go into your house, and . . . and I was just curious."

Trevor studied me for a long time. "Was this part of your zombie patrol? Did you think you'd find zombies in my basement?"

"Of course not," I said. "No way, dude. I . . . don't even believe in zombies."

"But I saw you with your friend in the graveyard. . . ."

"Alec? Alec believes in zombies. I don't," I said. "I told you, Trevor. I came down here because I was curious. That's all. We watched your movers and —"

"You were spying on me?"

"No. Really," I said. "We were . . . excited. Someone new moving in next door. So we watched the movers for a little while."

He nodded. He still gazed at me as if he was trying to read my mind. "Well . . . now you've seen everything," he said softly.

"Uh, yeah," I replied. "Guess I'd better get home." I took a few steps toward the stairs.

Trevor stepped up behind me and placed a bony hand on my shoulder. "Sorry, Kenny," he said in a low growl. "You won't be going home tonight."

I spun around. "Excuse me?" A stab of fear made me freeze.

"You won't be going home tonight — or *ever*," Trevor whispered. "You've seen too much."

34

A chill ran down my back. "What are you — ?"

Trevor tossed back his head and laughed. "Kidding," he said. "I was joking. I had to get you back. I mean, you broke into my basement."

"Sorry about that," I muttered.

"You still think I'm a zombie or something — don't you? Admit it, Kenny. You still think I'm a scary guy."

"No. No way," I said, trying to cover up my fear. "I . . . was just surprised, that's all."

He chuckled some more.

I couldn't wait to get out of there. What a frightening night.

I didn't realize that Saturday night would be even scarier.

I didn't tell my parents about sneaking into Trevor's house. But I did tell Grandpa Mo.

That next morning, I found him alone in the

kitchen, having his usual hot oatmeal and grapefruit. Mom and Dad had already left for their jobs.

I grabbed a glass of apple juice and sat down across from him at the breakfast table. He didn't look good. He gazed at me with red, watery eyes. The skin on his cheeks appeared to be dry and peeling.

"Grandpa Mo, you stayed up very late last night," I said.

He lowered his spoon to the bowl. "How do you know that?"

"I saw your light on," I said. Then I told him the whole story of what I found in Trevor's basement and why the coffins were down there.

He shook his head and mumbled something to himself.

"What's wrong?" I said. "I thought you'd be glad to know the new neighbors are okay."

"Yes, that's good," he said after a long pause. "Very good. But still . . ." His voice trailed off.

"Still?" I said.

He wiped his wet eyes with his fingers. "It's getting late, isn't it? You'd better get ready for school."

I started to stand up. Tricia burst into the room, dressed for school in a red-and-white sweater and a short black skirt over black tights. "You both look so serious. What are you two talking about?" she demanded.

"The football season," I said. "Same old Lions, you know?"

She squinted at me. "Since when are you into football?"

"I'm not," I said. "I was lying."

She slapped the back of my head as she walked to the kitchen counter. "Do you want cereal or toast?"

"I want peanut butter and jelly on toast," I said.

"Then make your own," she said. "I always get sticky peanut butter all over my fingers."

"That's why most people use a knife," I told her. I thought it was funny, but she didn't laugh.

I turned back to Grandpa Mo. He had that weird, faraway look in his eyes again. He was shaking his head and mumbling to himself. His oatmeal was only half-eaten.

He raised his eyes to me. "The zombie threat isn't over," he said. "I'm an old man, but I know what I'm saying."

As soon as I got to school, I told Alec about what happened at Trevor's house. "I guess we were wrong about him," I said.

"I still think the dude is weird," Alec replied. "But I guess we can cross him off the Zombies to Be Watched list."

Saturday night, he and I went out by ourselves on another zombie patrol. I talked to the other four guys and gave them a chance to change their minds and come with us.

But they said they were going to a *Star Trek* movie at the mall. They said they were over zombies. Zombies were old news.

As if *Star Trek* wasn't old news?

"They'll be sorry when they see us on TV talking about our zombie encounter," Alec said. "They'll be sorry when we're famous."

But we had a boring night — at first. I mean, we ended up just walking around and not seeing anything at all. Maybe it was because we decided to save the graveyard for last.

We started at the elementary school and patrolled the playground. Some high school kids were racing bikes back and forth on the soccer field in the dark. You're not allowed to have bikes on the soccer field. But Alec and I weren't going to tell them that.

The basketball court was lighted. A tall kid in shorts and a gray hoodie was all alone, practicing free throws. He was missing a lot and mumbling to himself.

"The school is zombie-free," Alec said.

I shook my head. "We'll never get on TV this way," I muttered.

A few blocks past school, TanglePark Woods begins. It's like a forest. It stretches for blocks. I'd never walked in it.

I swept my halogen light along the bare trees

at the edge of the woods. All was still. Nothing moved. Somewhere to the right, I heard the scrape of footsteps over dead leaves. Probably a deer or some other animal.

"I don't think we'll patrol the woods tonight," I said. "Too quiet."

"Zombie-free," Alec said. It seemed to be his phrase of the night.

Actually, our whole patrol was zombie-free. We gave up a few blocks past the woods and turned back for home. I shivered. The late-night air was damp. It felt cold enough to snow.

I stuffed my hands into the pockets of my down jacket. Alec whistled a tune I didn't recognize. He's a pretty good whistler. We didn't say anything. We both knew this patrol was a waste of time.

An SUV rolled by, filled with teenagers. Rap music blasted out of the open windows. They honked their horn at us as they sped past.

"They're having fun," I muttered. "Maybe we should have stayed at my house and played *The Walking Zombies*."

"Yeah. We would have seen more zombies that way," Alec joked.

We turned onto Ardmore. A few minutes later, the graveyard came into view. Beyond the iron fence, the gravestones glowed dully under the silver moonlight.

We were nearly to my house when we saw something going on in there.

Who were those people huddled around that tall gravestone? So many people together in the graveyard at night?

"Oh, wow," Alec muttered. He pressed his hands to his face as he stared. "Oh, wow."

And then the scene came clear to me, too — and I uttered a shrill cry of horror.

35

I could see four or five people circling the tall gravestone. They were walking strangely. Stiff-legged. Their arms hung at their sides.

My flashlight was on, but I decided not to shine it on them.

"Let's go closer," I whispered to Alec. "I can't really see them."

He nodded but didn't reply. We both edged across the street and stopped outside the tall iron fence.

I peered through the bars. And let out another cry because now I could see their faces clearly. I could see their decayed, rotting faces. Patches of skin missing on their cheeks and foreheads. Jagged teeth poking from their lipless mouths.

"Oh, wow," Alec repeated in a hushed whisper. "Oh, wow."

Their clothes were ripped and shredded. Their feet were bare, and I could see the bones . . . the bones of their toes jutting out from the rotting skin on their feet.

Some had skeletal hands. Two of them had dark holes where their eyes had been.

"Zombies." The word slipped from my mouth. "Dead people. Living dead people. We really found them."

I gripped the bars of the fence with both hands. Frozen in fright, I kept my eyes on the lurching, stiff figures. Moving in silence, they staggered around the tall, narrow tombstone.

And then they pulled another figure out. Someone had been hidden by the tombstone. Two of the ugly creatures had their hands on the man's arms. They jerked him roughly away from the grave.

"Whoa. Who's that?" Alec choked out. "Kenny, look. They've caught someone. It looks like . . ." His voice trailed off.

The zombies surrounded the man. I pressed my face against the bars of the fence, trying to see more clearly. I recognized the white hair first. And then his pale face came into focus.

"Oh, noooooo!" The horrified cry burst from my throat. "It's Grandpa Mo! They've got Grandpa Mo!"

36

I didn't wait. I didn't think. I pushed away from the fence, turned, and started to run full speed toward the cemetery gate. Panting like an animal, I heaved open the gate and raced inside.

Alec ran close behind me. Our shoes thudded the soft ground. I raised a fist and screamed at the zombies. "Let him go! Let my grandpa go!" My voice came out in a shrill, terrified cry.

I shook both fists in the air as I ran. I wasn't thinking about my safety. I wasn't thinking at all. I only knew I had to get my grandfather away from the hideous creatures.

The zombies turned at the sound of my cries. Grandpa Mo's mouth dropped open. He lurched toward me — but bony hands held him back.

"Let him go! Let him GO!" I screamed so loudly, my throat ached.

As I came closer, the smell of death swept over me. The thick, sour odor that rose from the zombies made me gag. They watched me approach.

One man's face was divided in two — half skin, half bone. The one next to him had an eyeball dangling from a gaping socket.

A tall zombie held on to my grandfather. The creature's shirt had rotted away. So had the skin on his chest. I could see his rib cage.

"Let him GO!" I screamed again.

Alec hung back. "Kenny — no! You can't fight them!"

Three of the undead creatures lined up in front of Grandpa Mo. They formed a wall to keep me from reaching him. The one in the middle opened his mouth wide and growled at me. He had no tongue.

"Kenny — go back!" Grandpa Mo choked out. "They . . . they . . . they are hungry. Very hungry."

"I . . . won't let them hurt you!" I screamed.

"You . . . can't . . . stop . . . them . . ." Grandpa Mo replied in a hoarse cry. "Go back! Go home!"

"No!" I cried.

The zombies grunted and growled like animals. One of them shook a fist at me. He had only two fingers on his hand.

Before I could back away, he lurched toward me. He grabbed my arm. He brought his face close to mine, so close I could see the tiny white worms crawling in and out of the skin on his cheeks.

"N-noooo," I uttered. "No. Please . . ." I tried to squirm free.

But he held on tight. And then he raised his hand with only two fingers. And slowly, he slid a bony finger down the side of my face, down my cheek.

Chill after chill ran down my cheek.

He snapped his teeth hungrily. A ragged tongue licked the spot where his lips had rotted away.

With a cry of horror, I broke free. I staggered back.

Alec had been paralyzed with fear. But he reached out and caught me before I fell.

"Grandpa Mo —" I gasped.

The three big zombies still formed a wall in front of him. I couldn't see how I could get to him.

And then, led by the two-fingered creature, all five zombies began to stagger toward me. They stretched out their ragged, bony arms, waving their skeletal hands in front of them. And lurched forward, lurched toward Alec and me.

"Run, boys!" Grandpa Mo called. "Run! It's too late for me. Save yourselves! They're hungry!"

I took a step back and bumped into Alec. My heart beat so fast, I thought my chest would explode. The grunting creatures moved slowly toward us, waving their hands in front of them, glassy eyes wild, reaching . . . reaching for us.

"Grandpa Mo — this is your chance!" I cried. "Run!"

But he stood watching the hungry zombies move in on Alec and me.

They dragged their bare, bony feet forward. The putrid odor rose off them, more sickening than any garbage pile.

"Run, Grandpa Mo!" I shouted one more time.

But the poor old guy seemed frozen on the spot, frozen in fear.

The grunting zombies were just a few feet away. Grabbing for us . . . stretching their decayed arms . . . reaching out for us.

I didn't want to leave my grandfather there. I knew the hungry zombies would eat him. But Alec and I had no choice. We had to save ourselves. We had to turn and run.

Our shoes slipped on the dew-wet grass. We leaned into the wind and darted away. We knew we could outrun the slow-moving creatures. But what about Grandpa Mo?

Alec and I stopped at the gate. Breathing hard, we spun around and looked back. I could see the zombies moving off with my grandfather. They didn't come after us. They just wanted to chase us away.

And now, they surrounded Grandpa Mo. They pressed against him. Formed a tight pocket around him so he couldn't escape. Lowering their heads. Lowering their heads to eat him.

"We have to save him!" I wailed. "We have to *do* something!"

But what could we do?

37

"Let's get your parents!" Alec cried. "Hurry — your parents!"

But I wasn't thinking clearly. I wasn't thinking at all. My grandfather was being eaten by zombies. My brain felt about to explode.

I took off running after Grandpa Mo. My shoes practically flew over the ground. Panic made me run faster than I'd ever run.

What did I plan to do? I didn't have a plan. I just knew I had to go back for him and try to pull him away from the hungry, undead creatures.

"No — Kenny! Stop! STOP!"

I felt Alec's hands on my shoulders. He gripped me tightly and forced me to stop running. "We . . . have to get help," he wheezed. "We can't . . . we can't do it on our own."

I gazed straight ahead. We had stopped at the tall tombstone. The tombstone the zombies had circled. The one they had hid Grandpa Mo behind.

Gasping for breath, I squinted at the front of the stone. Squinted at the words engraved there.

"Oh, nooooo," I moaned.

The words were faded, almost totally worn away. I couldn't read the dates of when the person was born and died. But I could read the name on the gravestone clearly.

MARIO MANZETTI

Another low moan escaped my throat. I moved closer to make sure I was reading the name correctly. Yes. Yes, I was.

My body froze in a chill of horror.

Alec stepped up beside me. His eyes followed my gaze to the tombstone. "Kenny? What's wrong?" he asked.

I pointed. "Mario Manzetti," I said. "That's my grandfather. That's Grandpa Mo."

38

Alex's mouth opened but no sound came out.

"Grandpa Mo died," I said in a trembling voice. "This is his grave. Don't you see? He wasn't *captured* by the zombies. He's *one of them*."

"But —" Alec stared openmouthed at the name on the stone.

"That's why he was so obsessed with zombies," I said. "That's why he knew so much about them. Because he *is* one."

"But he was afraid of them." Alec was finally able to speak. "Don't you remember, Kenny? How terrified he has always been."

"That was to keep us from guessing," I said. "But this explains why he went out at night. Why he came to the graveyard. To visit his zombie friends."

My voice cracked. "I . . . I can't believe I've been living with a zombie! I . . . I can't believe we've been going out on stupid patrols when the zombie was there the whole time — right inside my house."

Alec turned to me, eyes wide with shock. "Do you think your parents know?"

"I don't think so," I answered. "I have to tell them — right now."

I took one last glance at the name etched on the stone. Then I turned and started trotting toward the house. Halfway to the gate, I turned back. "Alec, are you coming with me?"

"No," he called. "I'm going home. I . . . I . . ." He couldn't explain. He turned outside the gate and darted toward his house. I didn't blame him. He wanted to be safe. He didn't want to be in a house with the walking undead.

I stumbled up the front steps to the house. I banged my knee hard. But I was too insane to feel the pain.

I struggled with the front door. Finally pushed it open and burst inside.

The house was warm and smelled of coffee. I could hear the TV on in the den. My parents always stay up late on Saturday night watching old movies.

Tricia? I remembered Tricia wasn't home. She had a sleepover with a friend from school.

"Mom! Dad!" I screamed, running to the den. "I need help!"

They sat close together on the leather couch.

Dad had his arm around Mom's shoulders. The room glowed from the bright TV screen.

They both sat up with a jerk as I hurtled into the room. "Mom! Dad! It's Grandpa Mo!" I cried.

"Kenny? Where've you been?" Dad demanded, climbing to his feet. "What's going on?"

"It's . . . Grandpa Mo," I choked out. I was panting too hard to talk. "He's . . . in the graveyard. He —"

"Again?" Mom cried.

"He must have had another bad dream," Dad said. He hurried past me, heading to the front door.

"I'm coming with you," Mom said.

"No. Wait —" I said. "You don't understand."

"We'll bring him home," Dad called from the front door. "Stay here, Kenny. We'll go get the poor guy."

They ran out, and the front door slammed behind them. I had no chance to explain. No chance to tell them the truth about Grandpa Mo.

I thought about running after them. But they told me to stay home. I stood there shaking, with chill after chill running down my body. I'd had enough horror in the graveyard for one night.

I climbed the stairs to my room. Slowly, my heart began to beat normally. My breathing slowed to normal, too. But every time I pictured the name on that old gravestone, my pulse started racing again.

In my room, I pulled off my jeans and shirt, still cold from the chill night air. I found my heaviest, warmest sweater and a fresh pair of jeans. Then I walked to the window and peered out at the graveyard across the street.

The moon had disappeared behind clouds, casting the ground in darkness. I couldn't see Mom or Dad. And I didn't see Grandpa Mo. Squinting into the blackness, my eyes swept back and forth over the cemetery. Nothing moved now. No one there.

I was still gripping the window ledge, peering out my window, when I heard the soft footsteps on the stairs. I whirled around and shouted. "Mom? Dad? Is that you?"

No answer.

I shouted again. "Did you find him? Did you find Grandpa Mo?"

No reply. Soft footsteps moving slowly up the stairs.

I whirled around and ran out into the hall. "Who's there?" I called. I crept to the top of the stairs.

And gazed down at Grandpa Mo as he climbed the steps, slowly, steadily. He raised his eyes to me. "Kenny." My name came out in a hoarse groan. "Kenny. *There* you are."

I gripped the top of the banister and watched him. I suddenly couldn't breathe.

His eyes appeared to glow as he stared up at me. His jacket was open, revealing a stained turtleneck sweater underneath. He climbed another stair. Stopped for a second. Climbed another stair.

Closer. Coming closer. Not taking his eyes off me. Coming for me. Coming to get me.

"Kenny . . ." he groaned.

"Grandpa Mo — I know the truth about you," I blurted out. "I . . . I saw the tombstone. I read the name. I know, Grandpa. I know."

He didn't stop climbing. "I'm so sorry," he rasped, his face suddenly menacing. "I'm so sorry you saw it, Kenny."

39

He reached the top of the stairs. He stepped onto the landing.

His eyes were suddenly sad. "I'm so sorry you saw it," he repeated. He grabbed me by the shoulders.

"No, please —" I cried.

How could this be happening? How could I be terrified by my own grandfather? What did he plan to do to me?

"I'm sorry you saw it, Kenny," he said. "That must have been a terrible shock. Let me explain."

I squirmed free of his grasp. "Explain?"

He nodded. His white hair fell damply over his forehead, covering one eye. He brushed it back. "You must have been so shocked and frightened," he said softly. "I'm so sorry."

"But —" I started.

"That tombstone . . . ," he said. "The name you saw . . . That was my *father*."

"Huh?" A cry of surprise escaped my mouth.

"Yes. That's my father's grave," Grandpa Mo said. "He was Mario Manzetti. I'm Mario Manzetti Jr."

I stared at him, my chest heaving. My whole body trembling.

"My father was killed in the war," he continued. "World War Two, back in 1944. I was just a boy. About your age, actually. His body ... It was brought back to Franklin Village and buried across from his house. This house. That's my father's grave across the street, Kenny."

I still couldn't speak.

"Did you think it was *my* grave?" He patted my shoulder. "That must have given you a real scare."

"I — I didn't know what to think," I stammered.

Grandpa Mo sighed. "This house has seen a lot of sadness," he said. "When my dreams started, I couldn't tell what was real and what was a dream. That's why I had to get away. I went up to Alaska. I was there for years. I didn't tell anyone in the family where I was. I was trying to escape my nightmares."

"Sorry," I muttered.

"But I couldn't escape," he said. "My nightmares about zombies. They followed me. They wouldn't leave me alone. In my dreams, the zombies wanted me. They were waiting for me in a secret tunnel. They were waiting to come up

155

from the tunnel and pull me down to them. Such a frightening dream."

He sighed again. "That's why I moved back to this house. To try to figure everything out. But tonight . . ."

"Those zombies in the graveyard were real," I said. "And they captured you. How did you get away from them, Grandpa Mo?"

He shut his eyes. I knew he was seeing them again in his mind. "I couldn't sleep," he said. "I went out for a walk. I walked past my father's grave — and they surprised me. They jumped me. They came out of nowhere."

"Were they the zombies from your dreams?" I asked.

He shook his head. "I didn't know them. They were hungry, see. After they chased you and your friend off, they led me away. They planned to devour me."

"Eat your flesh?"

He chuckled. "They were desperate. But not *that* desperate. I have no flesh left. Look at me, Kenny. My body is down to nothing but bone."

The old guy was right. He was pretty much a skeleton already.

"So, they let me go. Then they hurried off to look for food."

"We . . . have to tell Mom and Dad," I said. "We have to let them know —"

156

"They won't believe us," Grandpa Mo said. "Besides, I don't want to scare them away. They didn't want to move here, Kenny. Your parents hate this town and they hate this old house. But they decided they need to take care of me. If you tell them about the zombies across the street . . ." His voice trailed off.

"I won't tell Tricia, either," I said. "But what if —"

I stopped because we heard the front door open. "Kenny?" Dad called. "Are you okay? We couldn't find my father."

"I'm up here," Grandpa Mo called down. "I'm here with Kenny. Sorry if I gave you a scare. I'm perfectly safe."

Mom and Dad peered up at us from the bottom of the stairwell. "You're perfectly safe, Pops?" Dad said.

Grandpa Mo nodded. "Safe and sound."

But, of course, we *weren't* safe at all. This frightening night was just the beginning of the zombie horror.

40

"Is Franklin Village the scene of a horror movie come to life? Has the much-talked-about zombie apocalypse started right here in our town? I'm Bryan Reynolds for Eyewitness News. And I'm here with local police officer Maynard Welles, who has a frightening story to tell."

I turned up the volume on the TV. Tricia and I were in the den. She was on the couch, reading a book she had to do a book report on. This news report made my heart skip a beat. But she didn't look up.

"Kenny, could you turn that off? I'm trying to read."

I waved at her to shut up and turned the volume up some more.

Officer Welles was a chunky, red-faced guy in a red-and-yellow Hawaiian shirt. He spoke in a hoarse, raspy voice: "I was off duty. Coming home from seeing some friends. I saw the zombies threatening the two women. It was in front

158

of an empty lot at Terrace and Main. At first I thought someone was making a movie. You know. It looked like that TV show everyone is nuts about. *The Walking Zombies*."

The reporter broke in: "But then you realized the two women were really in trouble?"

"Some of my fellow officers don't believe me," Welles said. "But these zombies weren't guys in costumes and makeup. These guys were the real thing. When I got close, I could smell them, and I could see their bodies were all rotted and decayed. It made me sick. Seriously."

"Are you a zombie fan?" the reporter asked.

Welles shook his head. "No way. Especially after last night. I mean, I was as scared as the two victims."

"What did you do?"

"I didn't have time to call for backup or anything," Welles replied. "I knew I had to act. I shouted a warning, but they ignored me. Then I just started fighting them. I hit them. But they didn't seem to feel any pain."

"Because they were already dead?"

Welles nodded. "I think so. But they let go of the victims. Then the zombies turned and ran. I chased after them. I chased them to the graveyard on Ardmore. I watched them sink into the ground. Into open graves, I guess. Down into the dirt. Then I just stood there. Talking to myself. I think I said, *What did I just see?*"

Tricia grabbed the remote and clicked the TV off. "Give me a break, Kenny. I have to read this by Monday."

I tried to swipe the remote back, but she swung it out of my reach. "Tricia, did you see what they were talking about? Real zombies right here in Franklin Village."

She rolled her eyes. "Kenny, do you believe everything you see on TV? It's two days till Halloween. Of course they are doing stories like that."

"But that guy was a cop —" I said.

"You've been hanging out with Alec too long," she said. "Hey, did you finish down in the basement? You were going to move the chairs, remember? And finish stringing up the black-and-orange crepe streamers?"

I stared at her. My mind wasn't on the streamers. It was on my night in the graveyard with those zombies. My face suddenly tingled where that zombie had run his finger down my cheek.

"Maybe we don't want a zombie party," I said. "Maybe we should change the theme."

"Are you crazy? It's way too late," Tricia replied.

"But maybe we don't *want* dozens of zombies invading our house," I said.

She narrowed her eyes at me. "Go away," she said.

So ... that's just what happened. Two nights later, dozens of zombies invaded our house.

41

"What were you worried about?" Tricia asked. "This party is awesome!"

She brushed back the bloodstained veil and straightened her shredded wedding dress. Half her face was bloodred, and she had painted black circles around her eyes to make it look like the sockets were showing.

"I've counted four zombie brides here tonight," she said. "But tell the truth. Who looks the most undead? Me — right?"

"Right," I said. "You definitely look undead." I was glad Tricia was having a good time. Most of the zombies who crowded our basement seemed to be having fun.

Even Alec, who knew how terrifying zombies could be, was having fun. He even agreed to dance with Tricia, which was pretty amazing. Alec wore a red cap that made it look like his head was bleeding. And he had a skeleton hand poking out of one sleeve of his dark-stained white shirt.

The music was loud. So loud my parents decided to stay upstairs and not join us. The pizza was good. Everyone seemed to like the orange cookies and cupcakes.

Candlelight flickered inside the evil-looking jack-o'-lanterns we had carved. And I'd hung a bunch of cardboard bats from the basement ceiling. The basement looked like a real party room, a party room crammed with zombies.

It was an awesome party. I guess I was the only one who wasn't enjoying it.

I kept studying the faces of the costumed kids as they came down the basement stairs. I had a feeling *real* zombies might crash the party. Why? I guess because of the zombies we saw across the street. Or maybe because of Grandpa Mo's warnings.

The party was supposed to be a way to make new friends. But I was so tense, so worried that real zombies would burst in, I couldn't relax. I couldn't talk with anyone.

I jumped when a guy came down the stairs with his shirt ripped away and his rib cage showing. But as he stepped into the light, I saw that he was a kid wearing a skeleton T-shirt.

The next kid down the stairs had eyeballs dangling from his forehead. I asked him how he glued them on. He said they were real. Then he grunted and pretended to bite my shoulder.

It was funny, but I just couldn't laugh. My whole life, I never believed in zombies. But I definitely did now. And I definitely didn't want to see any tonight.

I was happy to see Grandpa Mo come down the stairs and join the party. "I won't stay long," he said, gripping the banister with his bony hand, taking it one step at a time. "I just want to see kids having fun."

"Awesome," I said. "Come sit down." I took his arm and led him through a group of kids. Then I shooed kids off the couch and motioned for Grandpa Mo to sit down.

"No. Wait," I said. "The couch is too close to the dancers." I motioned for Alec to help me. We each took an arm of the couch and we slid it back a few feet, away from the dancers. It wasn't easy. It was a really heavy, old couch.

"Thanks, Kenny," Grandpa Mo said. He turned and started toward the couch.

I spotted something on the floor. A square cut into the floor. It took me a few seconds to realize that when we moved the couch, we had exposed a trapdoor in the basement floor.

"Whoa!" I cried out as the trapdoor sprung straight up.

Who pushed it open? Could someone be *under* the basement?

Without thinking, I moved to the opening and peered down.

To my shock, I saw a girl. A girl with short blond hair. She raised her face to me — and my stomach lurched.

Her cheeks were eaten away. Her green eyes had sunk deep in their sockets.

Before I could back away, the girl shot up both hands — hands with bone poking out of the skin. She wrapped her hands around my ankles. Tightened them ... Tightened them ... And with a furious jerk, started to pull me down into the hole.

42

"No! Let go!" I screamed.

The music was so loud, I don't think anyone heard me. Kids were dancing all around me. No one even turned around.

I struggled to kick my legs free. But the girl was incredibly strong. She gave another hard tug. My shoes went over the edge — and I started to fall.

"Somebody! Help me!" A frantic cry rose from my throat as I slid down.

I glimpsed a rope ladder in front of me. I grabbed for it with both hands.

I struggled to pull myself up the ladder and back to the basement. But the girl held on with her skeletal hands. I fell to the bottom with a hard *thud*.

I saw that I'd landed on a dirt floor. Darkness all around. I seemed to be in some sort of cave or tunnel. The only light came washing down from the open trapdoor.

The girl pulled me to my feet. Her hair was in

matted clumps. Her eyes were deep in her skull. She had a short pointed chin. But her nose was gone. Just a rotted hole in her face. She reminded me of an elf. An undead elf.

She held me against the wall with both hands. And brought her face close to mine.

"No — please!" I cried. "Please — let me go!"

She smelled like rotting meat. Her lips were torn. Her front teeth were missing.

"Mario," she rasped, "don't you remember me?"

"No. Wait —" I gasped.

"Mario, it's me. Ivy. Your friend, Mario. Your friend who you left down here with the zombies. I've been waiting for you. I've been waiting a long time for you."

"No. You — you've made a mistake," I choked out. "You —"

Her fingers tightened around my arms till I wanted to scream.

"Mario, why did you leave me down here?" she demanded. "Why did you forget me? Why did you run away and leave me to the zombies?"

"N-no. I didn't," I stuttered. "It wasn't me. I'm not Mario. Listen to me —"

"Mario, I told you I'd have my revenge. You look so good." The torn lips formed a ragged smile. "You look good enough to EAT!"

Holding me against the wall, she lowered her face to my shoulder — and opened her mouth for the first bite.

43

I shut my eyes and waited for the pain.

But before she clamped her teeth shut, I heard a voice above us.

"Ivy? Is that you?"

She raised her head and spun around. We both saw Grandpa Mo slipping and struggling his way down the rope ladder.

She held me against the wall and squinted at my grandfather as he stepped forward.

"Ivy? It *is* you, isn't it?"

"Who are you?" she demanded.

"I'm Mario," he said. "Don't you remember me?"

She uttered a growl. "*This* is Mario!" she cried, motioning her head toward me. "Think I don't recognize Mario? Mario is *my* age."

"I — I'm not —" I gasped.

"That's not Mario," Grandpa Mo told her. "Yes. He looks a lot like me when I was twelve. But that's Kenny. He's my grandson."

Her torn mouth dropped open. She loosened her grip on my arms. She turned from me to face Grandpa Mo.

"Nooooo!" she wailed. "You're not Mario. You're OLD! You're too OLD!"

"But, Ivy —" Grandpa Mo pleaded. "You're still young because you died down here at twelve. But I —"

"I've waited for you all this time," she said to Grandpa Mo, her voice trembling. "All this time. But now you're old. You're too old!"

She tore at her scraggly hair with both hands. "Too old! I don't want you, old man! I don't *want* you! I want *Mario*!"

A shrill scream tore from her throat. She spun away from both of us. Still screaming, she staggered away, into the darkness of the tunnel.

Grandpa Mo and I stood there, staring into the darkness. I could still hear her screams far in the distance.

"Let's go," Grandpa Mo said softly. He gave me a boost up the rope ladder. I made it to the top, reached down, and helped him up.

He shook his head. "So *that's* what I've been dreaming about all these years. Ivy. That horrible day all those years ago with Ivy . . ."

Still shaking his head, he said good night and made his way out of the basement.

I let out a long sigh. I could still feel that zombie girl's bony fingers around my ankles. Still see her half-eaten face.

"Where've you been?" Alec's question broke into my thoughts. "Kids were looking for you."

"You wouldn't *believe* where I've been," I said. I started to tell him — but a loud scream made me jump.

Another shrill scream rang off the basement walls. Kids stopped dancing. More screams shattered the room.

I turned — and saw the grunting, open-mouthed zombie staggering across the room. And another hideous undead creature pulling himself up from the rope ladder.

The trapdoor!

"Oh, nooooooo!" A wail escaped my throat as I realized my horrible mistake. I'd left the trapdoor open.

And now the zombies . . . The hungry zombies from the graveyard . . . They were climbing up . . . into the room . . . into my house!

I'd let them into my house.

Drooling, groaning, reaching out with their rotted, skinless hands. They backed our screaming guests against the basement wall. Backed them against the wall, scraped, and staggered, and shuffled toward them, moaning . . .

"*Hunnnngry . . . Sooooo hunnnnngry . . .*"

Tricia stormed toward me. "Kenny? Is this *your* idea? Your little joke is *ruining* the party." "It . . . it's not a joke, Tricia," I stammered. "Then *do* something!" she shouted. *Do something?* What could I do?!

44

The zombies formed a ragged line. They snapped their jaws up and down hungrily as they moved in on my helpless, screaming guests.

Suddenly, I had an idea.

I pulled Alec away from the others. "The Zombie Goop Loops," I choked out. "Remember the dog in the graveyard? Maybe the zombies will like them, too."

Alec slapped at the sides of his costume. "I don't have any, Kenny," he said. "I didn't bring any to the party."

My hands trembling, I searched my pockets. No. None.

But then I glimpsed the food table against the wall. Yes! Of course! We put out two huge bowls of Goop Loops for the guests.

"Help me!" I cried. I pulled Alec to the table with me. I motioned to the Goop Loops bowls. We each picked one up. We ran across the room and burst in front of the attacking zombies.

"Hungry!" I shouted, waving the bowl under their noses. "Hungry!"

I tossed a few Goop Loops on the floor.

Would they go after them? Would they like them enough to give my guests time to escape?

I tossed a few more on the floor.

And waited. Waited.

It seemed like hours.

Finally, the zombies moved. They dove to the floor. Grabbing the loops in their skeletal fingers, they shoved them into their gaping mouths. They rolled over each other, wrestled, fought each other for the blue-and-red candy pieces.

"Yesssss!" A scream of triumph burst from my throat.

I dumped more loops on the floor. The zombies scrambled hungrily after them on all fours. They stampeded over each other, ripping at each other's faces and arms, desperate to grab up the candy.

Alec and I moved toward the open trapdoor.

"Hungry!" I screamed. "Here! Hungry!"

I turned the bowl over and dumped the Goop Loops into the opening. Alec raised his bowl and poured all the candy down the hole.

Grunting and growling, the zombies dove headfirst into the opening. They pushed each other out of the way . . . Snapped at each other . . . Wrestled and fought their way down through the trapdoor to the tunnel below.

Alec and I waited till the last zombie took a dive through the hole. Then we slammed the trapdoor shut.

"Hurry," I cried. We grabbed the ends of the big couch and slid the couch over the trapdoor.

"They're gone!" I shouted, pumping my fists in the air. Alec and I bumped knuckles. We both danced up and down in our excitement.

I turned to our guests. They clung to the wall, faces tight with fear, silent now.

Think fast, Kenny. You can save this party. Think fast.

"Did you enjoy that?" I asked everyone. "They were from the high school. We hired them to make this the scariest Halloween party ever. Weren't they awesome?"

A few kids laughed. A few cheered.

"Kenny, you're the best liar ever," Alec whispered.

I nodded. "I think they believe me." I turned back to the guests. "Crank the music up," I shouted. "Let's party!"

Tricia strode up to me. "Are you kidding me? You hired those high school kids? Seriously?"

"Seriously," I said. "Alec and I wanted to surprise you, too."

"Nice," Tricia said. "Their costumes were amazing. You guys really made the party exciting."

I wiped sweat off my forehead. "Glad you enjoyed it."

If she only knew the truth . . .

I saw three new people walking down the basement stairs. I crossed the room to greet them. I was going to tell them they were late. They missed all the excitement.

But I stopped a few feet away when I recognized them.

Trevor? Trevor and his parents?

Did I invite Trevor? Maybe.

But I didn't invite his parents.

"Hey," I called. "Glad you could come. But . . . you're not dressed as zombies."

Trevor strode up to me. His parents were close behind him. All three of them were smiling.

"You thought we were really zombies," he said. "When you saw the coffins, you thought we were zombies. But we're not. You were totally wrong, Kenny."

"I . . . I'm glad," I said.

"We're not zombies," Trevor said. "We're vampires."

All three of them opened their mouths. Their long, curled fangs slid down their chins. They raised their arms and moved quickly into the room, and my guests began to scream again.

GOOSEBUMPS MOST WANTED

SPECIAL EDITION

Ho-ho-horror!

THE 12 SCREAMS OF CHRISTMAS

Here is a sneak peek!

Gray clouds covered the afternoon sun. The air felt cold against my face. Two fat crows perched on the fence at the back of the yard. They cawed loudly as Ned and I ran and skipped over the tall grass.

We took turns hopping over a stack of firewood logs. We pulled open the door to the narrow garden shed. It smelled of fertilizer inside. A rusted wheelbarrow stood tilted against the back wall. Some kind of animal had chewed a ragged hole in one of the floorboards.

"What about that shack over there?" Ned said, motioning toward it with his head. "Let's look inside it."

The little shack reminded me of a gingerbread house my grandmother made one Christmas. It was a perfect, square little house — until Flora accidentally sat on it. She crushed one whole side of the roof. Ma turned it around so the crushed side didn't show.

The shack behind the garden shed was falling down, too. It was probably built before our house was. But it had gone to ruin. A lot of the shingles were missing. Green moss covered one wall. The window beside the entrance was cracked.

Ned started running to it, but I held him back. "Pa said not to go there," I said. "He said it might be haunted. That's what he heard in town. Something bad happened in there. And now it's haunted. That's why no one has lived in there for lots of years."

A smile spread over Ned's face. His dark brown eyes flashed. "It's haunted, Abe? Let's go!" he exclaimed. "Let's chase out the ghosts."

He was always braver than me. I couldn't let on that I was afraid of ghosts. Dad used to tell us ghost stories before bedtime when we were Flora's age. Ned loved them. But hearing about headless ghosts returning from the grave to find their head, or restless spirits that clanked and howled at night — hearing those stories gave me nightmares.

Ned picked up a long stick from the grass and walked toward the old shack, pretending the stick was a cane. I followed close behind, my eyes on the broken window and the darkness beyond it.

As we stepped into the shadow of the little house, a chill swept down my back. My skin tingled. Were there ghosts inside? Were they friendly? Or did they hate intruders?

About the Author

R.L. Stine's books are read all over the world. So far, his books have sold more than 300 million copies, making him one of the most popular children's authors in history. Besides Goosebumps, R.L. Stine has written the teen series Fear Street and the funny series Rotten School, as well as the Mostly Ghostly series, The Nightmare Room series, and the two-book thriller *Dangerous Girls*. R.L. Stine lives in New York with his wife, Jane, and Minnie, his King Charles spaniel. You can learn more about him at www.RLStine.com.

Catch the
MOST WANTED
Goosebumps® villains
UNDEAD OR ALIVE!

scholastic.com/goosebumps

**Available in print
and eBook editions**

GBMW7

NEED MORE THRILLS?
GET Goosebumps! ™

WATCH
ON TV
ONLY ON
hub

PLAY
Wii

Nintendo DS

Goosebumps HorrorLand

Goosebumps

ON DVD

Goosebumps GHOST BEACH

Goosebumps ATTACK MUTANT

LISTEN

Goosebumps HorrorLand

Goosebumps HorrorLand

Goosebumps HorrorLand
DISC 1
REVENGE OF THE LIVING DUMMY
R.L. STINE

Goosebumps HorrorLand
ESCAPE FROM HORRORLAND
R.L. STINE

SCHOLASTIC
www.scholastic.com/goosebumps

2GO

R. L. Stine's Fright Fest!
Now with Splat Stats and More!

SCHOLASTIC

www.EnterHorrorLand.com

GBHL19B